The Secret Life
of a
Teenage Siren

The Secret Life
of a
Teenage Siren

WENDY TOLIVER

Simon Pulse
New York London Toronto Sydney

SIMON PULSE
An imprint of Simon & Schuster Children's Publishing Division
1230 Avenue of the Americas, New York, NY 10020
Copyright © 2007 by Wendy Toliver
All rights reserved, including the right of reproduction in whole or in part in any form.
SIMON PULSE and colophon are registered trademarks of Simon & Schuster, Inc.
Designed by Ann Zeak
The text of this book was set in Garamond 3.
Manufactured in the United States of America
First Simon Pulse edition December 2007
10 9 8 7 6 5 4 3 2 1
Library of Congress Control Number 2007933816
ISBN-13: 978-1-4169-5065-3
ISBN-10: 1-4169-5065-6

For Lynn Gray:
my mom,
my inspiration,
my hero

Acknowledgments

I am grateful to my editor, Michelle Nagler, for her enthusiasm and patience, and to Caroline Abbey for championing my book from the get-go. I'm so lucky and honored to work with the amazing people of Simon Pulse. I want to thank my fabulous agents, Christina Hogrebe and Annelise Robey, who not only believe in me, but make me believe in myself. Big hugs to my CPs: Aryn, Nadine, Jennifer, Denise, Kaylie, and the Eden Writers' Circle. Thanks to Drienie and Kwana for always being "on call"; and Marley, an angel on Earth. A shout-out to my parents and my sister and brother for their infinite love and support. Last but never forgotten are my three sons, Miller, Collin, and Dawson, whose bright blue eyes and mud-splattered faces remind me of what really counts; and Matt, who stole my heart and will never let go.

One

I want to kiss Zach Parker. Just once. Is that too much to ask?

I pretend like I'm getting a kink out of my neck so I can sneak a quick peek at him. His Denver Broncos cap is shadowing his eyes, but they're this baby blue color and they're simply heavenly. He's got wavy, sandy hair that almost reaches his shoulders, and on the rare occasions that he's not wearing a cap or a football helmet, it's always falling into his eyes. He's tan already, and I doubt he's ever had to buy a tube of Clearasil in his life. Some girls think he looks like David Beckham, but I think he's even cuter. Oh! He glances at me and I swear our gazes lock for a split second of heart-stopping ecstasy (on my end, any-how). I whip back around and look straight ahead, accidentally making eye contact with the teacher. Wonderful.

"I take it you're finished with your quiz, Roxy?" Mr. Hickenbaum asks, stalking over to my second-row desk.

"Um, no. Not quite yet."

"Then maybe you should keep your eyes on your own paper and stop looking at Zach's."

Oh my God. The entire English class swivels in their seats to stare at me. Eva "the Diva" Nelson and her trusty, busty sidekick, Amber, laugh in the way only cheerleaders with freakishly large lung capacity can.

I wish I could say, "If I were to cheat on a quiz, which I most certainly did not, I wouldn't rely on a *jock* for my answers." But I'm not that brave. And I'd have to be stupid to talk smack about jocks, since Zach, J.T., and Devin are all sitting in the back row. Even if they're juniors and this is a class for sophomores.

Eva raises her hand and I sink into my chair. "Mr. Hickenbaum, it's obvious Roxy wasn't trying to cheat off Zach's paper." My ears perk up. Can it be? Is the Proud Crowd

Queen finally being halfway nice to a band geek (or a BeeGee, as we're fondly referred to at Franklin) like *moi*? "She was just trying to get his attention. You know, to see if he has a date to J.T.'s party tomorrow night. Right, Roxy?"

The classroom explodes into laughter and I'm sure my face is as red as a cherry. This can't be happening. Please, God, make this all be a terrible nightmare. You know, one of the ones where you go to school and everything seems normal till you look down and realize you're wearing nothing but your little brother's Sponge-Bob SquarePants slippers?

Mr. H marches back to the front of the room in his Dr. Scholl's, whips around, and fixes Eva with an icy glare. "Thank you for enlightening us, Miss Nelson." Then he turns his back to us and writes, HAVE A NICE SUMMER BREAK on the blackboard in big yellow squeaky letters.

I hear a few hopeful gasps as I gnaw on my pen cap. It would be my luck to have him cancel a quiz that I'm acing.

"Don't forget to recycle your quiz on the way out." Mr. H crosses his arms over his Michelin Man chest and smiles benevolently as his students grab their backpacks and file out.

When I get to my locker, my best friend, Natalie, is already there. She sweeps her brown flippy hair off her face and stuffs her flute case into her Eastpak. She's wearing her new last-day-of-school outfit—a short, flirty skirt and an embroidered tank. If teachers ever gave quizzes on the latest issue of *Lucky*, she'd get straight As.

Natalie could almost qualify for a legit Proud Crowd member. I mean, she passes on two very important requisites. One, she's got a closet full of cute-slash-expensive clothes. Two, she's demented enough to think she's a chub, never mind she weighs a hundred and ten pounds even in her chunky Steve Maddens. But like me, Natalie's a BeeGee, and that little detail is a mega deal breaker.

Eva and Amber saunter by, side by side. I swear, those two are joined at the hip. And they must share a brain, too, since each only has half. "Cute bebe shirt," Eva the Diva drawls in passing.

Natalie's chest puffs up just a hair. "Thanks!"

Amber stops to examine the tank top.

"I had one like that when I was in junior high."

And just like that, my friend's face crumbles like the last Cinnamon Twist in the Taco Bell bag. After the queen and princess of the Proud Crowd float away on their strappy sandals, Natalie whispers, "It's vintage. But Amber wouldn't know that, now would she?"

I shake my head as if I know the difference between a shirt that's vintage and one somebody dug out of a fifty-cent box at a garage sale. "So, we still on for tomorrow night, then?"

"You betcha. Can't wait, birthday girl!" She gives me a little kiss on my cheek. "Well, I'd better get going. Dad's picking me up any minute now." She slings her purple backpack over her shoulder and scurries down the hall.

Natalie's dad lives in Colorado Springs, and she visits him every other Friday. So we're not really celebrating my Sweet Sixteen till tomorrow. Natalie and I are going to T.G.I. Friday's and then to the movies. Her treat, it being my birthday and everything. We really want to see that new Orlando Bloom movie. You know, the one where there's a glimpse of his naked butt? Anyway, it's not like my plans are super-exciting, but hey. I'm looking forward to it.

Having a birthday dinner with my family, like I'm doing tonight, is as exciting as watching nail polish dry. *Clear* nail polish. Maybe I should look on the bright side, though. Could this be the year my birthday wish will come true? Maybe I'll finally get my first kiss. Well, my first *real* kiss. You know, with a guy, on the mouth . . . maybe with a little tongue? With Zach Parker, perhaps?

Somewhere in the hallway, I hear Zach's voice. I've had a crush on him for so long, my ears are fine-tuned to his voice's frequency. I blow my bangs out of my eyes and suck my stomach in, a routine that's become more of an instinct than a conscious effort. Just as Zach and the other jocks strut around the corner, Alex McCoy sidles up to me and lays his big trombone case next to my Skechers.

Alex sits behind me in band, tooting his trombone, his face pink and jolly. Come to think of it, he sits behind me in every class we have together, and his face is pink and jolly whether he's blowing into his trombone or not. Alex and I live in the same neighborhood, and since I don't have my license yet, he drives me to school. Which is cool of him, but I wish I could be carpooling with Zach instead. But, like I've already said, Zach's a jock. And not only does he play football, baseball, *and* soccer, but he's the crown jewel of the Proud Crowd: a two-time Homecoming attendant and the reigning Prom Prince. Sure, people might say he's out of my league, but a girl has to set her expectations high.

"Hey, Rox. You about ready?" Alex asks, but I ignore him so I can hear what the jocks are saying. "Oh, here's your yearbook back," he continues. "Sorry it took me so long to sign it."

I snatch my yearbook from him and jam it into my backpack, ears tuned to the jocks' convo.

"No, dude. She's spent way too long in the fake baker. Totally not my type," Devin says. I don't really know much about Devin, except that he's one of Franklin's best athletes.

Then Zach says, "How about Lindsay Lohan? Man, she's hot. Definitely *my* type."

Lindsay Lohan? I'm assuming he means circa *Mean Girls* and not Rehab Girl. But anyway, I look nothing like the beautiful movie-slash-pop star. For one, I have frizzy red hair. I have microscopic boobs and eyes the color of mud. That is, if you can tell through these thick glasses I have to wear. My nose is covered with blackheads, and I swear my right leg's longer than my left.

The world's best makeup, hair, and wardrobe team couldn't make me half as beautiful as Lindsay Lohan. My only hope would be Photoshop, where I could merge a photo of me with one of her and then airbrush to no end. But that's beside the point. Fact is, Zach Parker would rather be with someone beautiful and famous than someone . . . well, someone like me.

"Need any help with that?" Alex asks, nodding at the pile of school crap that I've stopped stuffing into my backpack.

"Hurry up, J.T.," Devin calls over his shoulder. I sneak a peek at Zach's butt as he and Devin strut down the hall. Man, all those sports are definitely paying off.

J.T. bumps my arm when he's getting a football out of his locker. "Sorry," he mutters under his breath. J.T. is the jock I know the best, probably 'cause his locker's next to mine. Lots of girls think he's all that, but I find the whole unibrow thing a bit creepy. I'm convinced that J.T. stands for "Just Trim it."

"It's okay." I stoop down to pick up my backpack, and Alex grabs our instrument cases.

J.T.'s looking at me all weird. Then he grins and asks, "So, are you coming to my party tomorrow night?"

Am I hearing things? Did J.T. just ask me to a Proud Crowd party? *Me?* "Er, no . . ."

"Why not? I'm getting a keg and everything."

"Okay, maybe." Or maybe *not*. Sure, a jock just invited me to his party and maybe I should be stoked. Natalie would be so into it, she'd make a special trip to the mall to buy the perfect outfit. But I have a feeling this invite is nothin' but bad news. And even if it isn't an evil get-the-BeeGee-here-so-we-can-make-her-life-a-living-hell plan, I don't want to be anyone's charity case. Not even Zach Parker's.

"Cool." J.T. tosses his football high up into the air and catches it.

I slam my empty locker. "Cool."

Alex mutters, "Cool," even though he's not even in the conversation.

J.T. jogs off, yelling to the other jocks,

"Hey, Zach! You've got a date for the party!" and all the other kids in the hall turn and stare at me, mouths agog.

Just kill me now.

I duck into the passenger seat of Alex's gray Civic. It smells like cinnamon apples, courtesy of the red paper tree dangling from his gearshift. Ever since Alex got this car, he's had a red tree in here. He must've bought a mondo box at Costco or something.

I click on my seat belt. Instead of starting the engine, Alex just looks at me. His light brown eyes are wide open, making him look kinda cute, in a puppy dog way. Natalie's always saying Alex has a Zac Efron thing going on, and though their hair and eye colorings are totally different (Alex is blond-and-brown, not brown-and-blue), maybe she's onto something. "You okay?" he asks, offering me some Skittles.

I pop a purple one into my mouth and shrug my left shoulder. "Fine. No biggie." I'm just now noticing that he's wearing a yellow bowling shirt and army-green cargo shorts. I might not be a fashionista like the

Proud Crowd chicks or Natalie, but even *I* know his getup registers a negative score on the style meter.

We haven't said a word the entire drive, which is kinda weird because Alex always has something to say. "Is something wrong?" I ask, once we're at my house. "You're acting like the Paxil poster child."

"Do you have a thing for Zach Parker?" he asks out of the blue.

I shrug casually, but I feel my face heat up like an atomic fireball. "Not really. Well, sort of. I mean, I don't really know him all that well."

I replay the scene at my locker in my mind, like I've been doing ever since it happened. God, I just can't believe J.T. *said* that. You know, about me being Zach's date. First Eva, then J.T. I swear, humiliation is like quicksand. The more I try to get out of it, the deeper I sink. Deeper and deeper—oh, God. Is that a zit on my chin? Seriously, all this stress is doing nothing to help my complexion issues.

"I thought Natalie liked him."

"*Every* chick at Franklin likes him," I say, adding a silent "Duh."

"Oh."

"Hey, Alex? Can I ask you something . . . personal?"

"Uh, okay."

"We're friends, right?"

"Yeeees. But that's really not that personal, Rox."

"No! *That's* not the question. I'm just making sure you'll be completely honest with me. Because friends are completely honest with one another. Don't worry about hurting my feelings. I just want . . . a guy's view." Oh, great. It *is* a zit. Right in the middle of my chinny-chin-chin.

He squirms in his seat and fiddles with the air freshener. "All right. I'll tell you the truth."

"Cool, thanks." I take a deep breath. "On a scale from one to ten, one being mirror-shattering hideous and ten being . . . oh, let's say someone like Lindsay Lohan . . . what am *I*?"

"I don't know, Rox." He stares at the dash. "I don't really feel comfortable ranking people like that. It's not like I can just assign a number. It's just—"

"I get it." I fumble with the door handle.

He reaches out and touches my shoulder.

"I . . . Okay. Here goes." Now his face is more green than red. "A nine."

I open the door and jump out. "A nine? As in just one away from a perfect ten?" I frown at him and cross my arms over my A-cups.

"You're a ten when you're smiling." A tiny grin flicks across his lips.

"I'm no nine, Alex. You're just trying to be nice. I told you to be *honest*." I slam the door and head for my house, my glasses slipping down my nose with every stomp. I hear Alex get out of the car, but I don't stop.

"Rox!"

"Good-bye, Alex. Thanks for the ride."

I'm so sure. I ask Alex to be truthful and he has to be all nice and everything. If a girl asks for honesty, she wants it to be at least *somewhat* believable. If he'd told me I was a five, for example, I might have believed him. But a *nine*? Ha! Only in a parallel universe where frizzy hair and zits are the stuff of supermodels.

I run inside and toss my backpack and flute case on my bed. The house is a virtual graveyard, like it always is when I get home from school. It's actually pretty nice 'cause I get to have a little time to myself.

The doorbell chimes. Pumpkin, Mom's beloved Pomeranian, scampers down the hall to the front door, yipping enthusiastically. I follow behind, wondering if it's Alex. Maybe I should invite him in for a snack or something. I mean, it's kind of ridiculous for me to get all mad just because he was being nice. That's just Alex, Mr. Nice Guy.

Really, he's one of the sweetest guys I know. He's such a great friend, but sometimes I wonder if . . . well, what if he *was* being honest about me being a nine? In his eyes, I mean.

There's a cheery knock on the door as it's opening. "Yoo-hoo, birthday girl!" An elegant, manicured hand emerges and pats Pumpkin on the head three times. He immediately shuts his yapper and bows his foxlike head, making way for Grandma Perkins.

As much as I love her, I'm in no mood to have my cheeks squeezed by this lady who looks more like she's my mother than my grandmother. Agewise, anyway. She hogged all the Beauty and Talent genes, leaving Mom and me with the Good Personality leftovers. And we don't even have *those* when we're PMSing.

Grandma doesn't come over very much. For one thing, she and Mom don't get along all that great. I guess it's 'cause they're so different from each other. But the main reason I never see Grandma is she's never, ever home. She's always off doing something glam. Like going to some dude's condo in Hawaii, for example. Or cruising the Caribbean on another guy's yacht. Last month she hooked up with a trio of French men who gave her a private tour of Western Europe. So, anyway, we're together so rarely, she sometimes forgets I'm not a little girl anymore, like she's in a time warp or something.

Come to think of it, I bet she gives me another freaking Barbie doll for my birthday. Can you imagine? A Barbie for a sixteen-year-old! I never got into Barbie, even when I was six. But Grandma Perkins made sure I'd never have to endure a shortage of proportionally unrealistic plastic dolls.

Grandma Perkins shuttles her grocery sack to the kitchen and returns clutching her big sparkly handbag. She raises her hand to my face, and I wince. For the first time ever, she doesn't pinch me. She brushes a piece of hair off my cheek and smiles.

Her smile can make men fall to their

knees. It still amazes me that she hasn't landed a husband. She got pregnant with Mom when she was twenty, but she never married the guy. Men fall all over themselves to date my grandma, but she rarely goes out with the same one twice. Now that's what I call picky.

Or maybe it's just the lifestyle she grew accustomed to when she was a jazz singer. If you've never heard of Gertrude Isabel Perkins, don't sweat it. She was famous back in the Stone Age. Ah, well. Who am I to judge? If anyone is retreating into spinsterhood with grace and aplomb, it's Grandma Perkins.

She checks her watch, a diamond Cartier that a lovesick businessman gave her "just because." She frowns slightly and takes my arm. "You were born at exactly two fifty-four, sixteen years ago." Interesting. So she *does* know I'm sixteen. Mom must've clued her in.

She then asks, "Does your watch say 'two fifty'?"

I glance down at my polka-dot pink watch, the one I got on clearance at Target. "Yeah. Why?"

Grandma Perkins puffs out her cheeks

and shakes her head. Her shoulder-length, light blond hair floats around her face like she's in a Pantene commercial. "Only four minutes, and then we'll know. Come with me." She drags me into the bathroom, locks the door, and sits me down on the toilet seat.

I try to stand up, but she's pressing down on my shoulders with unbelievable strength. "What are you doing?" I ask. She's studying my face like she's never seen me before. Oh no! Don't tell me she's got dementia or Alzheimer's or something. "What's gotten into you, Grandma? Are you taking some new kind of meds?"

She loosens her hold a bit and offers me a small smile. "How do you feel, dear? Do you feel light-headed or anything?"

"No, why? Do *you*? You're acting totally weird . . ." Oh my God, is she having a stroke? A heart attack? Is she *dying*? I've got to get to a phone. I've got to call Mom or 911 or Dr. Phil or somebody. I bolt up off the toilet seat and try to get past her, but she blocks the door with her five-foot-nine, model-svelte frame.

"Just two more minutes. Give it just two more minutes," she says, her voice a touch raspy.

I perch on the edge of the tub. I'm not sure what's going on, but I'm freaking. Is she hiding out from her latest boy toy or something? It wouldn't be the first time. Or maybe she's some sort of gangster or a cat burglar. I mean, how she lives such a glitzy lifestyle is a major mystery. It's not like she has a job or anything. Could the cops be on their way? Or the FBI? Or that dude from *America's Most Wanted*?

She reaches out and grabs my upper arms. "It's time."

My heart is beating so hard against my rib cage, I swear it's gonna shoot right out of my body. Suddenly I feel tingly. Like when my foot's asleep and the blood is rushing back in. Only it's all over my body. I can't help smiling. I can't help giggling. "Ha-ha-ha!" My voice sounds so distant and tinny in my own ears, like I'm in Eisenhower Tunnel. "Ha-ha!" There goes that weird laugh again. And what's that smell? It smells like the beach, like ocean water in here.

Oh, God. I can't see. Everything's so . . . blurry. *Blink, blink, blink.* It's not helping! I take off my glasses and examine the lenses. They're a little scratched up, but they're clean. Well, as clean as they ever are. What's going on? After rubbing my eyes, I scan the bathroom. Weird. Everything is clear. I can see without my glasses!

Huh?

Grandma Perkins's beautiful lips curl into a smile and she takes a step back. Tears glisten in her emerald green eyes as she gazes at me. Quietly, she says, "Take a look in the mirror, Roxy."

Still feeling rather punchy, I do as I'm told.

Oh. My. God.

TWO

I gawk at my reflection. My fiery red hair is now a shiny, sleek, gorgeous mane. I take a few steps back, shake it upside down, and flip up again. Not a hair out of place. Where has my frizzy, crooked-banged, 24/7 bed-head hair gone?

And it's not just my hair. I jump up on the counter to get closer to the mirror. My eyes are as green as Grandma's and my skin is so dewy and flawless, I look like I just stepped out of a Neutrogena ad. My lashes are lush and curly, and my nose is blackhead-free. Oh! And that zit on my chin has mysteriously disappeared. I smile and see that my teeth are dazzlingly white.

I'm having a hard time breathing, like

when I wore that corset for Halloween last year. When I look down, I see why. My bra (a glorified training bra) is all but busting at the seams. Holy cleavage! I can't help but give my round, perky C-cups a quick squeeze. Wow.

"Grandma?" My voice wavers. "What's going on? Did you give me some kind of hallucinogen?"

"Of course not, honey. And to be frank, your references to drugs are making me a bit nervous. Remember, just say no to drugs."

I study my reflection in the mirror. This is all so bizarre. "So if I'm not hallucinating, what's the deal?"

"You're going through The Change. It's your time."

The *Change*? Before I can explain to her that I've already gone through puberty (thank-you-very-much), she drags me away from the mirror and whisks me down the hall. "We mustn't dawdle," she says. "Your parents and brother will be home soon, and we have so much to talk about."

A nanosecond later we're in my bedroom with the door locked and the blinds closed. She digs in her handbag and produces a wrapped gift. Aha. The perfect size for one of those collectors' edition Barbies. She lowers herself gracefully onto my bed. "Take a load off, honey," she says, patting the daisy-patterned bedspread. "This is a day you'll never forget."

I raise a now-elegant eyebrow, stealing a peek at myself in my bureau mirror. Still gorgeous. What the hell's going on?

She hands the gift to me. "What I'm about to tell you is going to change your life forever. Open it, Roxy."

I pluck off the violet bow and stick it on my head (old habits die hard). Then I tear the pale green paper to find an ancient, leather-covered book. "Oh, I get it. The Barbie's inside, huh?" This must be the way they package the really expensive Barbies. Maybe Grandma got me this one in Rome or something.

Grandma's left eyebrow rises. "Oh, honey. I know you're disappointed that it's not a doll. But you're not a little girl any-more." She pats my knee. "Most people grow out of the Barbie stage by now."

Not a Barbie? Who is this woman sit-ting on my bed?

I run my fingers over the cover of the book. I try to read the title, but it's written in some strange, curlicue language. The pages are thick, with shiny bronze edges that might have been gold at one time. "A Bible?" I guess. "A scrapbook?"

She laughs—a beautiful, fluttery sound. "No, no. It's *The Enchiridion of the Seirenes*. But I just call it *The Siren Handbook* because that's what it is."

"The *what*?"

"Roxy, you are a Siren."

"Come again?" I take the bow off my head, ripping out a few of my hairs. A few of my beautiful, shiny, straight, golden-red hairs.

"We're both Sirens."

"You can't be serious." I snort-laugh, sprawling out on my pillows. Did she get bitten by a rabid raccoon on the way here? A diseased prairie dog or a mosquito, perhaps? Or . . . is she telling the truth? After all, something very bizarre is happening here. Something I can't explain.

"Yes, honey. I'm serious."

"A Siren? You mean one of those mermaid things? If I jump in the water, will I grow a big fish tail?" I ask jokingly.

"Actually, the original Sirens had the upper bodies of beautiful maidens and the lower halves of birds. Through the ages, the image has evolved, and now Sirens are oftentimes depicted as mermaids. But we've evolved even further, and as you can plainly see"—she gestures up and down her pink-and-black Chanel suit—"we don't have any fish or bird body parts. Just beautiful woman parts."

It takes every ounce of self-control not to slap my forehead. What am I supposed to say, "Oh, that's cool. 'Cause I'm allergic to feathers, and scales don't do anything for my complexion"?

"So let's just pretend that we're having a completely sane conversation," I say when I finally find my voice. "I guess my next line would be something to the effect of 'Cool! I've always wanted to be an imaginary creature thought up by some dude in a toga.'?"

Sirens are imaginary, right? They aren't real. And I most definitely am not one. Feathers and scales aside.

She marches over to the bookshelf and slides out my Webster's. "Maybe this will help." Pacing around my room, she flicks through the pages and reads the definition out loud: "'Any of a group of female and partly human creatures in Greek mythology

that lured mariners to _____
enchanting music.'" Sh_____
"Here's another one. 'A wo____
bewitchingly beautiful music; a ___
beautiful woman.'" She taps her fing___
the page. "Yes, yes."

As this is sinking into my mind, she sits
down on my bed and gazes at me all mushy.
Like how I'd imagine she looks at the puppies
at the pet store. Or the lobsters in the tank
at fancy restaurants. "My granddaughter is a
Siren."

Oh, God. She's the portrait of sincerity.
Grandma Perkins truly believes I'm a Siren.
I swallow, contemplating what to say next.
I guess I'll just go with the flow. Test the
waters, so to speak. At least it'll make her
happy. And maybe, when she comes back to
the real world, we can just pretend like none
of this happened.

"You didn't know until today?" I ask.
"That I'm a Siren or whatever?"

Her green eyes twinkle. "I had my sus-
picions. You have so much beauty on the
inside, you just needed for the outside to
catch up."

"Why didn't you tell me?" I ask, lifting
the leather-bound book onto my lap. "If I'd

had even a chance of becoming out gorgeous, it would've saved me a lot of pain growing up. Do you have any idea how many times I've been called Pepperoni Face? Peppermint Patty? Band Geek of the Week?" I can go on and on. . . .

"I *couldn't* tell you, dear. It's one of the two rules. We cannot tell a soul. If we do, we lose our Siren powers. Of course, if you someday have a daughter or granddaughter who becomes a Siren, you can mentor her, as I'm doing for you." She rocks back and forth gently, a wistful look in her eyes. "My mother told me I was a Siren on my sixteenth birthday."

I never knew my great-grandmother, but I've seen pictures. She was one of the most elegant, beautiful women I've ever seen—sorta like Nicole Kidman but not as pasty. "So your mom was a Siren, then you . . . and now me? What about Mom?"

She leans in so close I can smell her minty breath. "The Sea Nymph gene is passed down from mother to daughter, but occasionally it skips a generation or two to help ensure that we're not discovered."

"Does Mom know you're a Siren?"

"No."

"Will she know *I'm* one?"

"I'll come up with a cover for your physical transformation, so don't worry about that."

This is ridiculous, ludicrous, *crazy*. And yet Grandma Perkins looks so serious and so . . . happy. What's the harm in playing along for a bit longer? "You said the first rule is we can't tell anyone. What's the other rule?"

She takes a deep breath and squeezes my hand so hard I swear she's cutting off my circulation. "A Siren cannot fall in love."

This is getting crazier by the minute. "Can't fall in love? Why not?"

She takes *The Siren Handbook* from my lap and flips the pages until she finds whatever she's looking for. In a reverent, almost musical voice, she reads: "'Once a woman becomes a Siren, she cannot fall in love. Whilst she can enjoy camaraderie and liaisons with the men she encounters along the journey of life, she is forbidden to bequeath her heart. Like the Sirens of Greek mythology, Sirens of today have irresistible yet deadly allure. If a Siren allows a man to get too close to her, he shall live just a moment more in pure ecstasy and then suffer a horrific, untimely death.'"

I peer at the book as she's reading, and, like the title, there's just a bunch of mumbo jumbo swirled on the page. It's as if a two-year-old got ahold of her mommy's calligraphy pen and went to town. I snatch the book from her and flip through the pages. "How can you read that? What language is it in?"

"The Sirens of past all had musical gifts. One sang, one played a flute, and one played a lyre," Grandma Perkins says. "My gift is singing. When I want to use my Siren powers to their fullest, I sing." She bends over and picks up my flute case. "I suspect your musical gift is playing the flute."

"Contrary to what Mom says, I'm not very good. I mean, I sit in the third seat, but that's only when Macey McMullen's got a sinus infection."

"Play your flute, and the words will come to you."

"So if I just play a little song on my flute, I'll be able to make sense of these markings?"

"That's right." After Grandma Perkins closes the book, she takes my hand and looks into my eyes. "Honey, I know this is . . . quite incredible."

I spring up off the bed and twist open the blinds. Gray clouds are gathering in the otherwise blue sky. Grandma Perkins's sporty little Lexus is parked in the driveway. Seems like she's always got a new car. "Are there other Sirens out there?" Maybe there's a Siren chat room. Or a Sirens Anonymous chapter around here.

"We can't be sure." She joins me at the window and puts her hand on my shoulder.

Fat raindrops splatter rhythmically on the street. "Because we can't talk about it to anyone but each other," I say. Of course. And it's not like anyone would believe us anyhow.

Grandma Perkins says, "It's for your own protection, honey. If the word got out, you and I would become living science experiments."

"Or we'd be on the front page of the *National Enquirer*, along with the vampire sheep and woman who gave birth to triplet aliens," I say with a laugh.

Grandma shrugs. "You never know. That's why it's so important that we keep it a secret." She studies her appearance in my mirror and smoothes her already perfect hair. Her eyes find mine in the reflection. "Now, you stay in here and learn about being a Siren. I'm going to start your birthday dinner." She gives my shoulder a couple of pats and then turns to leave.

This is all so ridiculous. I'm not a Siren. Grandma Perkins isn't a Siren. There are no such things as Sirens. Even the dictionary says they're some kind of creature from Greek mythology. They're not ordinary girls who go to high school in the Denver suburbs.

But how can I explain how I've turned from Plain Jane to Lindsay-Lohan-eat-your-heart-out in mere minutes? Unless my life has been one big Scooby-Doo cartoon and I've been wearing a band geek disguise for sixteen years, then maybe . . . possibly . . . *perhaps* there's a grain of truth to this whole Siren thing.

"Grandma?"

She turns around. "Yes, Roxy?"

"So, if I'm a Siren—"

"You *are*," she says softly.

I clear my throat. "So I'm a Siren and now what? I mean, what's the point?"

Her green eyes glow. "You've been

given a gift, and how you use it is up to you. This handbook will help you answer your questions. And you can always come to me, Roxy. Anytime." She winks at me and then closes the door behind her.

Can this really be happening?

Three

Cranking an old Black Eyed Peas CD, I dance around my room, taking every opportunity to catch glimpses of myself in the bureau mirror. I toss my hair from side to side and then bend over at my waist and flip back up. My gorgeous mane floats through the air like spun gold and then lands with every thick, luxurious hair in place. I sing along with Fergie, holding an imaginary microphone and striking Fergie-esque poses all over the floor. Wiggling hips, gyrating butt, palms pumping up in the air like a rapper, followed by a rather futile attempt at the moonwalk (just for kicks). Running back over to my bureau, I make all sorts of faces in the mirror: pouty sexy, wide-eyed innocent, nose-up conceited, tongue-out-and-cross-eyed crazy.

Keeping time with the music, I strip down to my underwear and jump up on the bed. Higher and higher, reaching for the ceiling, knees bending up into my chest. Spread eagle, hurky, 360, back-scratcher, *Fiddler on the Roof* dancer move—any kind of jump I can think of or make up. I leap off the bed like a rock star, landing on my floral rug in a pseudosplit.

Then I pull myself up and ransack my closet, tossing clothes and shoes onto my bed and all over the floor, looking for the perfect outfit to showcase my new Siren bod. I slip on four pairs of jeans, countless tops, a bunch of skirts, and a particularly bright and pouffy gown I got for 75 percent off at Nordstrom (just in case someone had asked me to a school dance last year), modeling each outfit as if my bedroom were a runway, complete with famous designers, a celebrity-studded audience, and an onslaught of camera flashes.

In a pink tank top with a silver dragon design and black shorts, I twirl around and around, using the mirror as my focal point like I learned in ballet class when I was eight.

Is that beautiful girl really me? Dizzy, I

flop onto my bed on my back, my knees knocking together, and my C-cups rising and falling as I try to catch my breath. Staring at the ceiling, I can't help but laugh. This is *off the hook*!

I run down the hall, hollering, "Grandma, I'll be right back!" and grab my bike out of the garage. I haven't ridden it in ages, but I guess it's true that once you learn how to ride a bike, you never forget. The wind whips through my fiery tresses as I pedal through the neighborhood, past all the pastel- and neutral-colored houses, up and down hills, through all the stop signs without even slowing down. I breathe in and out, the early-summer air sending warmth through my entire body.

A Jeep with three college guys stops in the middle of the street. They're totally staring at me. Not really sure what to do, I smile and wave as I ride by. The guys whistle and call out, "Hey, baby, you're so fine!" and "What's your name, gorgeous?"

My name is Roxy Zimmerman, I say to myself. Roxy Zimmerman the Siren.

I park my bike by my mother's Outback. Dodging Chase's camo backpack and his grocery bag of last-day-of-school stuff, I almost trip on Pumpkin, who's acting all excited to see me. "Settle down, boy! It's just me." I pat him on the head. His tail's wagging so hard I'm afraid it's going to fall off.

"Roxy, is that you?" my mom calls from the kitchen. When I turn the corner, I hear her saying, "It's just that I didn't know you were coming, Mother. But I'm glad you're here, really. What a pleasant surprise. And it smells wonderful. What are you making?"

Is Mom going to freak out when she sees me like this? And how in the world is Grandma going to explain my transformation? I mean, hel-*lo*, people don't turn from Plain Jane to Gorgeous Siren in the blink of an eye. This is real life, not Cinderella!

I hover by the entrance to the kitchen. Mom is digging in the fridge for something, her brown hair frizzed even worse than usual. "Happy birthday, Roxy!" she says cheerfully, a carton of lemonade in her hand. When her eyes land on me, her mouth drops open, revealing rows of silver fillings. Chase, who's sitting at the kitchen table, looks up from his bag of microwave popcorn, gawking at me like I'm an alien or something.

"Doesn't Roxy look lovely?" Grandma Perkins trills, beaming.

Launching out of his chair, he pushes through Mom to get a closer look. "Holy *shit*," Chase says, his cheeks chipmunked with all the popcorn.

Mom shoots him a glare that would make 50 Cent pee his pants.

"Those makeover artists in Palisades Square sure know their stuff," Grandma says, her green eyes twinkling. "I hope you don't mind, Merrilee, but I got Roxy out of school today and took her to the salon for her birthday gift. You only turn sixteen once!" She grabs a crocheted hot pad out of the drawer and heads over to the oven.

"But . . . but . . ." My mom licks her lips, apparently fumbling for words. "She looks like an entirely different person."

Grandma closes the oven and sets the timer. When she turns back around, she's smiling confidently. "It's about time someone brought out Roxy's best features, wouldn't you say?"

"Yo, Chase! Where are you, dude?" Porter, one of Chase's soccer buddies, tramps in and stops dead in his tracks. He's looking at me as if I'm a steaming hot Big Mac with extra pickles.

I twirl around like Julie Andrews in *The Sound of Music*. Mom says, "Roxy, you . . . you . . . are so beautiful." She hasn't taken her eyes off me since she first saw me as a Siren. And is that lemonade permanently glued to her hand or what?

I feel like dancing (well, I sort of am dancing). I feel like singing. I feel like knocking on Zach Parker's door and saying, "Look at me now!" And he'd take one look at me and say—

"She's freakin' hot!" Porter exclaims.

"Dude, she's my *sister*," Chase pushes his friend out the door. "That's just sick."

Dad has to work late tonight, as usual. When he stumbles over the threshold with a turquoise gift box, he takes one look at me and sticks his right hand out. "Hi, I'm Stan, Roxy's Dad."

"Dad, it's me," I say, shaking my head in disbelief.

The gift drops and crashes on the tile floor, right next to his size-twelve Sears specials. "Oh, yeah. Right, honey. I, uh, just, uh, thought you were a new friend . . . of yours. It's just been . . . a really long day. Sorry about that."

"It's okay. I know I look a little different than I did this morning." Poor guy. I've always felt sorry for engineer types. They're great with numbers and techie gizmos, but put them face-to-face with another human being and they can't string a coherent sentence together to save their lives. They can't dress worth a damn either, but that's another rant. My dad's only saving grace is his car. He drives a red Porsche Boxster. It's pretty old, but it's still one of the coolest cars in the neighborhood.

Dad loosens his überugly tie and swallows, his Adam's apple bobbing in his neck. "Did you have your hair done?"

"Something like that."

I grab his hand and take him into the dining room, where everybody's waiting. We all sit in our usual spots, and Grandma Perkins heaps food onto our plates. Baked chicken with lemon sauce, spinach salad, and almond couscous.

We don't talk all that much, but there's a lot of staring going on. I don't blame my family for wanting to look at me all night. I can hardly tear my emerald green eyes off my reflection in the window.

Dad, Mom, and Grandma Perkins sing "Happy Birthday," which sounds like a trio of Adam Sandler, Roseanne Barr, and Céline Dion. (Chase thinks he's too cool to sing.) I close my eyes and make a wish. This year, it's a no-brainer. I wish I really am a Siren.

Four

To be completely honest, I'd rather stare at my gorgeous self in the mirror than at the squiggles inside this so-called *Siren Handbook*. But I may as well get some questions answered. Plus, I admit I'm curious. What does this strange little book have to say about the new me?

I take out my flute and stick it together. I lift it to my lips and blow slowly. My bedroom fills with the most beautiful music I've ever heard. It's sort of new agey, like Enya, but way cooler. Actually, it sounds like the rain outside. Soothing and mesmerizing. Smooth as liquid. Sweet as a kiss. At least, how I'd imagine a kiss.

I rub my hand over the cover of the book

and in lavish script, the title *The Enchiridion of the Seirenes* appears like magic. Like something out of a Harry Potter book. Not that I've read one, but Chase is totally into them. Last year I had to chaperone him and two of his snotty-nosed minions at the bookstore for this big "Ode to Harry Potter" bash. They even dressed in black robes and round glasses. And he thinks *I'm* a geek!

Ah, well. Now I have my own magical book to read. I open it and start at the first page.

> Long ago, when legends were born, many a ship entered the Tyrrhenian Sea and drew near the infamous Anthemoessa Island, which was encircled by a wall of jagged black rocks. Beautiful, mesmerizing music wafted o'er the still waters and silent winds, enveloping the mariners like a soft mist. As they rowed even closer still, the sweet, melancholy, girlish voices of the Sirens took possession of their hearts and souls. Willing ears were promised that after a brief visit to the enchanting island, they would continue their journey not only charmed, but bearing

wisdom that only the gods possessed.

Alas, the men could not resist. They threw themselves into the deep waters and swam through the dark swell, their sights set on the mysterious Sirens who leaned over the crag, beckoning them closer still. The creatures they saw had angelic faces framed with long, silken locks, eyes as green as emeralds, and lips yearning for the kiss of true love.

Their encounter with the Sirens, the enchanting yet deadly sea nymphs, was so heavenly, the men entered the world of the dead with joyous hearts.

Wow. Talk about bizarre. What are Sirens, some sort of femme fatales?

There's a picture of a Siren on the facing page. I run my fingertip across it. Her hair floats around her head like the waves in the ocean. She's curvy, but not fat, and completely nude. The Siren sits on a rock, her bottom half covered in feathers. I'm about to turn the page, but something catches my attention. Something about the eyes. Though the picture is black-and-white, her eyes are a piercing green. I look even closer, holding the book up to my face. The eyes are shimmery, luminous, and breathtakingly beautiful. Two pools of emerald green water, gazing back at me.

A tap on the door startles me, and I slam the book closed, launching little sparkly dust particles into the air. I shove it behind my pillow and paint a bored-yet-innocent expression on my face.

"It's just me, Roxy," my grandmother says, peeping in. "Your father said he'd clean up, so I'm going to go home now."

"Grandma?" I sit up.

She comes in, closing the door behind her. "Yes, dear?"

"Is this for real? Are we truly Sirens?"

"Yes, Roxy."

"I've been reading this book you gave me, but it's just all this legend stuff. What does it have to do with twenty-first century me?"

"Do you have any specific questions?"

"What kind of powers do I have?" Actually, I've been wondering this ever since Grandma mentioned Siren powers, but I didn't want to come off all power-hungry. As if transforming into a total hottie in a matter of minutes wasn't enough.

"Your power comes in two parts, just like the dictionary definition," Grandma Perkins says. "Beauty and music. And, like our ancestors, our power only works on men. Your physical attractiveness will get you far on its own. It's no mystery that good-looking people have certain advantages over plain people." She lowers her voice before continuing. "But if you play your flute, the sky's the limit. If a man has something you desire— a job, money, a summer home in Greece—all you have to do is play a few notes and he'll bend over backward to make your every dream come true."

"All I have to do is play my flute and men will do anything I want them to?"

"Yes." She pauses a moment and then says, "Or rather, they'll do anything they *can* do. For example, you can't make a man without any artistic talent paint a beautiful portrait of you. But you *can* ask a male artist to paint a portrait of you free of charge, and it will be to the very best of his ability. While you can't make a man grow taller," she says, pointing to the ceiling, "you *can* get a short man to wear lifts in his shoes without a single complaint. Do you see what I mean?"

"Yeah, I think so." I close *The Siren Handbook* and place it safely in my drawer. "So I'll need to take my flute with me whenever I want to use my Siren powers?"

"If I were you, I'd have it with me at all times. One never knows when it will come in handy."

When I wake up the next morning, I reach over to my nightstand to grab my glasses, like I've done every morning since the fourth grade. But they're not there. Where did I leave them? Oh, right. The bathroom. And then I remember *why* they're in the bathroom. That's where Grandma Perkins held me prisoner while I transformed into a Siren.

Am I still a Siren, or was it all a really bizarre dream?

I sit up straight and blink once, twice. When I look at myself in the bureau mirror across the room, I just about scream in delight. Not a hair out of place. I look like Jennifer Aniston on a good hair day!

There's a knock on my door. "Honey, are you awake yet?" Mom asks, cracking it open. She comes in and perches on the edge of my bed. She's wearing a turquoise top and navy tennis skirt, her varicose-veiny legs stuffed into the whitest tennis shoes I've seen outside the shoe department. She leans over and rakes her fingers through my hair.

"What's up, Mom?" I ask, hoping she doesn't ask questions about my new appearance.

"I've got to leave for tennis now, but would you like to practice driving a little later on? Say, six o'clock? We could go on I-25 if you want." Monday's the big day. The day I get my driver's license. I haven't really driven very much with my learner's permit, so I admit I'm a little nervous about taking the test.

"Actually, I'm going out with Natalie tonight."

"Oh." She picks at a piece of lint on my comforter. "Well, okay. I'm sure you'll do fine on your test, anyhow."

"Yeah." How ever am I going to keep my being a Siren a secret from my own mother? And how did Grandma keep it a secret from her all these years? "Hey, Mom? I've always been curious, what exactly happened between you and Grandma? If you don't mind my asking . . ."

She brushes an imaginary wrinkle out of her skirt and then sits down on my bed. She sits there for what seems like a week, apparently sifting through her thoughts. "One day when I was about your age," she says, finally, "I asked her about my father. I had accepted that he wasn't ever going to be part of my life, but I still wanted to know at least *some*thing about him." She stares off into space for a minute and then says, "I figured it would help me know myself better."

"Can't you hire someone to find him?" I ask. "Or look him up on MySpace or Google him or something?"

She shakes her head. "Mother wouldn't tell me anything about him, not even his name. I begged her to show me a photo of him, but she said she didn't have any. The more I tried to get her to talk about my father and what happened between them, the more she closed herself off. She'd be anywhere but home, with anyone but me. And I guess I took it personally." Mom stands up and smooths the comforter where she'd been sitting. "But enough about that. What's in the past is in the past."

Wow. Grandma Perkins is so not normal. And I'm not just talking about the

Siren thing. What, does she want everybody to think my mother was an immaculate conception or something? What could be so bad that she'd keep it from her one and only daughter? One-night stand? Sperm donor? Nowadays, hardly anything is considered scandalous.

As Mom walks out, I can't help feeling sorry for her. It would suck to know absolutely *zilch* about your father. Sure, there are times my dad annoys me—he annoys the whole family sometimes—but I love the guy and can't imagine my life without him.

Once I hear Mom plodding down the stairs, I lock the door. Then I slide open my underwear drawer and unearth *The Siren Handbook*. Flopping back onto my bed, I run my hand over the leather cover. I turn each gold-rimmed page until I find where I left off. But before I can read another word, there's another knock on my door. I hide *The Siren Handbook* under the covers even though the door's locked. "WHAT?"

"What are you doing in there?" Chase yells. "Making out with your teddy bear again?"

I groan. "You wish." The kid learned

everything he knows about sex by watching *South Park*.

Giggling. Oh, great. There's more than one prepubescent pervert outside my door. "What are you doing, *really*?" Chase asks, jiggling the doorknob. "Why's the door locked?"

"To keep the scary monsters out."

"Open up already. Porter told everyone you're cute now and no one believes him, so he said he'd prove it and now everyone's waiting to see if he was telling the truth."

Wonderful. "How much?"

After a pause, Chase asks, "What do you mean?"

"How much money is riding on this bet?"

"Fifty bucks."

Whoa. That's a bunch, considering a twelve-year-old's allowance is about ten bucks a week.

"Okay, I'll come out in a little bit. But not until you all go in the basement like good little mutants and play Xbox so I can get dressed in peace."

Without a hint of grace, I roll out of bed. Then I carry *The Siren Handbook* over to my dresser, pull out a drawer, and hide it safely under all my underwear. I smile at my reflection in the bureau mirror, marveling my superwhite teeth. I can't wait to go out with Natalie tonight, now that I'm a Siren.

But I'm getting some bad vibes just about now. I mean, it's one thing to justify my new image to my family, but to my best friend?

Five

Thank God, it's 6:00 and Natalie will be here any minute. Chase's group of friends has multiplied like dandelions in a windstorm, and they've been trailing my every move. Each time I slipped into my bedroom to read more of *The Siren Handbook*, I'd find random twelve-year-olds stashed in my closet or under my bed.

I look out the window. Aha, there she is, Miss Promptness in the yellow Sportage. After grabbing the Old Navy satchel I found at the outlet last summer, I tug my jean jacket out of the overstuffed coat closet. "Don't be out too late, honey," Mom says as she kisses my forehead.

Chase's prepubescent posse begs me not to leave. I've had it. This is just too weird.

Even Pumpkin has taken to following me around—his tail waggin' and tongue hangin'. I swear, it's like I'm one of those doggie cookies Mom buys at the bakery and Chase's friends steal from the cookie jar, believing (for some unknown reason) that they're actually for *people*. Chase swears they taste like shortbread, but I'm not about to taste-test a doggie treat.

Anyway, if I were a walking, talking doggie cookie treat, it would make sense that the pipsqueaks and dog can't leave me alone. But I'm not. I'm something much more bizarre. I'm a Siren.

Oh! I almost forgot! I run back into my room and grab my flute case.

When I slip into the shotgun seat, fixing the spaghetti strap that keeps slipping off my shoulder, Natalie's chatting on her cell phone and doesn't even glance my way. Her tiny frame is stuffed into a plucky black sundress so small, she probably stripped it off her sister's Bratz doll. Her hair is flipped up even more than usual, and I catch a whiff of her Clinique Happy perfume. "I know, I know," she mumbles. "I'll do it tomorrow.

Yeah, I *know* it's important. I won't forget."
She rolls her eyes in a nonverbal "Get off my
case, meddlesome woman."

After she hangs up, I ask, "What was
all that about?" But I know it was her
mom, nagging her to get a job. I hate to
break it to Mrs. O'Brien, but Natalie has
no interest in a job. She already has a car
and a Visa card (thanks to her dad, who's
afflicted with Overcompensating Divorced
Parent Syndrome). Besides, a work schedule would only cut into her shopping time.

I, on the other hand, definitely need to get
a job. Especially if I plan on driving something besides Mom's ancient Outback wagon.
And that would only happen if she weren't
using it, which, between her job (she's a
kindergarten teacher), all her community do-
gooding, and tennis, isn't very often.

I guess I'll just apply for a job at
Wendy's. Looks like I'm destined to do the
"mustard, pickle, lettuce, tomato" mamba.
I mean, it's not like I have a college degree
yet, or any work experience besides baby-
sitting my brother when my parents go out.

Would Wendy's give me Saturdays off,
though? That's the day Alex and I get some
old folks from Willington House together at

the Pet Advocacy of Denver (PAD for short), which is a really nice dog pound that arranges adoptions and never puts unwanted pets to sleep. There's this circular sidewalk behind the PAD and the old people walk the dogs around and around all morning long. Alex and I came up with this little idea when we were at band camp, and the rest is history. We like to think it's a win-win situation for everyone. Except for Natalie. She's allergic to dogs (and old people, I suspect), so she graciously declined our invitation to come with.

Natalie turns to me and drops her phone on her lap. "Omigod, Roxy?"

I smile, but there are butterflies in my stomach. "My grandmother got me a makeover for my birthday," I say, borrowing Grandma Perkins's story. Too bad she's not here to help me right now.

Natalie twists her head from side to side, apparently searching for something. "Are we on some kind of reality TV show?"

"Uh, noooo. Why?"

"*Damn*, girl. I barely recognize you. What all did they *do* to you?"

"A little bit of everything, I suppose. They did a really good job, huh?" I keep smiling, not really knowing what else to say. To be honest, I'm afraid. Natalie reads all the fashion mags and watches TLC, so she sees professional makeovers all the time. She's gotta suspect something's fishy.

"You've got to get me an appointment, Roxy. I can't believe how great you look." She checks her reflection in the visor mirror and says wistfully, "I wish I had a mysterious, filthy rich grandma who'd pop out of thin air to make me into a hottie." She flips the visor up and her gaze settles on my chest. "Did your granny buy you a boob job, too?"

"I, uh, guess I just wasn't wearing the right bra," I say, slouching into the seat. "You know they say eight out of ten women don't wear the right bra size?" Okay, so I'm a crappy on-the-spot liar. Gotta work on that.

"Omigod, Roxy. Your eyes. They're so . . . green. Are you wearing those tinted contacts?"

"Um, yeah. The makeover people thought I'd look better without my glasses so I'm giving contacts a shot."

"Well, colored contacts are so last millennium, but they really do work for you. Hey, wait . . . I thought touching your eyeballs grossed you out." She's watching me warily, her nostrils flaring slightly with every breath. "I've been trying to talk you into contacts for years."

"Yeah, well, they're not as bad as I thought. I guess I should've listened to you." I smile at her, and promptly squash my lips together. Please, oh please, don't ask about my teeth. I can't squeeze out another single lie.

She shakes her head and switches her stereo to Y104, the same station we listened to when we were in junior high. An oldie by No Doubt is playing. Then she grabs a polka dot gift bag out of the backseat and hands it to me. "I hope you like it."

I reach into the bag and take out a Roxy shirt. It's chocolate brown with orange and white stripes on the collar. Natalie is the proud sponsor of my wardrobe. She never lets me forget that my name happens to be the brand name of a company that makes surf-slash-snowboard clothes and accessories. Every birthday, I can bank on her giving me a Roxy tee, beach bag, or visor. And every Christmas, a Roxy sweatsuit or parka. It was fun at first, but now it's anything but novel. I'd never say anything to hurt her feelings, though. We're best friends, and she means well.

"It's awesome." I peck her on the cheek and refold the shirt. "Thanks a bunch."

"You're welcome, Roxy. It's totally *you*. I knew you'd love it."

After she puts on her aviator sunglasses, we're off to T.G.I. Friday's.

"Sorry, ladies," the hostess singsongs. "There's, like, an hour and a half wait." Natalie and I exchange looks while she pops her gum.

"For just two people?" Natalie asks, exasperated.

The chick nods and then yells over the din, "Morton, party of eight, your table's ready."

"Well, forget it," Natalie says. "I'm just going to pee real quick and then let's try Chili's or something. Be right back, 'kay?"

"Sounds good." I sit down on the edge of a bench to wait. But Natalie doesn't move. She just stands there, looking around the waiting area and the nearby tables, her lips slightly parted. The boys and men are checking me out. Every single one in sight.

Am I giving an accidental panty peep show? I cross my legs, just in case. A handful of the guys blink, clear their throats, or loosen their ties. But I can tell they're still watching me. And so can Natalie. She shakes her head, her hair swishing side to side, and then drops her jaw. She's doing a remarkable impression of a goldfish.

"Well, no *wonder* they're all staring at you," she hisses. "You're carrying your freaking flute case. God, Rox. You might as well have a neon sign over your head that says LOOK AT ME! I'M A BAND GEEK! Hel-*lo?*" She knocks on my head three times. "It's Saturday night, it's summertime, and we don't have to be in band class for, like, three whole months. What are you thinking? Are you going to do a nice little recital while everyone's waiting for a table?" She rolls her big blue eyes as if I'm the most ridiculous excuse for a human being she's ever known. I do look rather ridiculous, I guess. And thanks to Natalie's impassioned monologue, I'm feeling mighty ridiculous too.

After an encore of her dramatic eye-roll, she turns on her heel and marches to the bathroom.

As I feared, everyone's still staring at me. A couple of college-age girls are even laughing. My cheeks blazing hot, I slump into the back of the bench, wishing I could pull a

Susan Storm and become The Invisible Girl.

But wait! If I use my Siren powers, can I get that manager over there to give us a table? I've already made a fool of myself in front of all these people. What have I got to lose, besides an hour and a half wait? Heart pounding wildly, I assemble my flute and raise it to my lips.

Beautiful, mystical music wafts through the onion ring–scented air. From where I'm standing, it looks like all the men who hear my song are swaying, gazing at me with post-Thanksgiving-dinner, sitting-in-front-of-the-TV, favorite-football-team's-winning eyes. The ladies, however, are scrunching their noses, whispering and pointing, apparently shocked to see a girl playing a flute in the waiting area of T.G.I. Friday's. One of the college-age girls is laughing so hard she'll probably pee her (very tight) pants, and the other just stood up and said, "I can't believe this. What a freak!"

Is this really going to work? When I stop playing, I still have everyone's attention. I smile at the manager and curl my finger, gesturing him to come over, all Siren-like. But I don't feel Siren-like at all. Maybe I *am* a freak. I'm about to run out the door, never to step foot in this restaurant for the rest of my life, but two seconds later the manager is right in front of me, apparently waiting for whatever I have to say. Oh my God. Here goes nothing.

I take a deep breath and he leans in, even closer. *You can do it, Roxy.* "Excuse me, do you suppose you can seat my friend and me right away? You see, we wanted to catch a movie, and the wait's awfully long, and . . ."

He takes my hand and escorts me to the hostess. "Carrie, make sure this young woman and her party are seated at the next available table."

She scowls and narrows her beady eyes at me. My flight mechanism revs up as she paints an obviously fake smile on her face. "Sure, Greg. Anything you say."

He does a little bow and tells me, "So sorry about the inconvenience. We're so honored you decided to dine here tonight."

"Oh. Well. Thanks." I take a deep breath and forge on. "It's one of our favorite places."

As the hostess extracts two menus from behind the podium, I overhear a woman ask her friend, "Did that girl just get seated before us?"

"Isn't she that famous flutist, er . . . uh, what's her name?" her friend asks.

The first lady says, "Famous flutist? Good heavens, Martha. What are you talking about?"

I've never, ever had anything even remotely similar happen to me. Typically, I'm the one who's stuck on the bench for well over the projected wait time. The forever forgotten one. This is totally weird, but totally exciting. My Siren powers really work!

And I'm glad, because I'm awfully hungry. If Natalie weren't paying, I'd order everything on the menu. Wait a minute. Could I use my Siren powers to get free food? I guess it's worth a shot.

I follow the manager into the kitchen, heads swiveling in my wake as I meander around all the tables. I push through the swinging doors and whip out my flute.

Half a dozen cooks, two dishwashers, and a random waitress make up my audience. The waitress glares at me and says, "You must be lost. We don't do the live music thing at T.G.I. Friday's. Try the bistro down the road," but I don't stop.

The manager is standing in front of me before I even finish my song. Hmm. How long do I have to play for the powers to work?

"Hi, me again," I say to Mr. Restaurant Manager, putting my flute away in its case. "I know this sounds kind of weird, but do you think you can give my friend and me all the free food and drinks we want? Just tonight, seeing as how it's my birthday." Well, technically, it's the day after my birthday, but what's he going to do? Check my birth certificate?

He does a little bow, never breaking his glazy gaze. "Of course, my dear. I'll take care of it."

Wow. Okay then. I give the rest of the kitchen people a little "thank you" grin and skedaddle.

By the time Natalie gets back from the bathroom, we've got a table by the window. "How'd you get us seated before all those people?" she asks, nodding at the crammed waiting area.

I shrug and replace the spaghetti strap that slipped off my shoulder. Stupid strap. "I guess we were the only party of two."

"But this is a table for four."

Again, I shrug, trying to appear as nonplussed as she is.

The bartender whips up some fruity mocktails he thinks we'll like, and in no time, our table is covered with a smorgasbord of food.

"So what did you get for your birthday?" Natalie asks, her mouth full of fried cheese. "Besides the rad shirt I just gave you."

"Let's see . . . my parents gave me a silver frame, but Dad dropped it so they're going to get me another one. Chase got me a dorky T-shirt that says *my little brother did it*, and Grandma got me a . . . er . . . makeover."

You know, being a Siren is one thing. But having to come up with all these lies really sucks. Does Grandma Perkins come up with stupid excuses like this? Or has she been a Siren for so long, lying comes naturally? Will it be easier for me when I've had some practice? And will it still bother me, or will I get so used to it, I'll forget what it's like to be completely straight with my friends and family?

"So, how was Colorado Springs?" I ask, shifting to a topic I hope I won't have to lie about.

"Same ol'," she says, haphazardly assembling a lettuce wrap. "I'm always with my dad, so I don't ever get to flirt with the Air

Force guys. But the good news is, he took me shopping and bought me a boatload of really cute clothes." She stuffs the wrap in her mouth and then licks the peanut sauce off her fingers.

"Need to hit the bathroom?" I ask, once we're done eating and drinking way too much. It's always nice to ask, just in case our bladders are on the same schedule. Unlike a lot of girls, Natalie and I are perfectly secure going to the restroom alone.

She says, "Nope, I'm good. I'll just wait here and get the check."

I hurry to the hall by the restrooms and plop down on a little bench. Framed black-and-whites of Hollywood movie stars cover the wall. A picture of Marilyn Monroe is right in front of me. She's wearing a cute white bathing suit, looking over her shoulder coyly.

I pull out my cell and dial Grandma's number. "Hi, Roxy. How are you? It's fun being beautiful, isn't it?"

Roxy Zimmerman, beautiful. Roxy Zimmerman, a hottie. A girl can totally get used to this. "Grandma . . . are you busy? Are you, like, on a date or something?"

She laughs her lovely laugh. "Of course

I'm on a date, honey. You don't expect me to pay for my *own* seafood dinner, now do you? I'm in a delightful five-star restaurant in Maine. I had a hankering for some lobster, you see, and it's not like Colorado—"

"Maine?" Just like that.

"Was there something you needed to know? Something about your . . . *birthday present*, perhaps?" I can all but see her giving me a long-lashed wink over the phone.

"Nothing important. Just a little bummed about having to lie to my best friend, you know, to keep it all on the down-low. I feel like a lying scumbag."

"Of course you do. I had the same concerns when I was your age." I hear a muffled, "James, my granddaughter is on the phone and I need a little privacy. Do you mind excusing yourself for a moment or two? Thank you." Next, in a hushed tone, she says, "You see, lying is perfectly acceptable because this is a very special case. It's a tip-top secret that cannot be leaked, no matter what the circumstances. If you blow your cover, you'll blow the cover for all of us—today and forevermore. If you tell anyone our secret, you will lose your powers." She continues in her regular voice, "That, my dear, is the sobering truth. So. Is there anything else I can help you with before the main course arrives?"

"Yeah, one quick question. How long do I need to play my flute for someone? You know, for it to work?"

"That depends, honey. I'd give it at least thirty seconds until you learn to recognize the signs that they're under your power. Each man is different, but most will get a peaceful look in their eyes, as if they're hypnotized. Men who are already under the spell of your beauty tend to be more susceptible and are quickly entranced, so they may only take twenty seconds or so. If you happen to use your Siren powers on the same man more than once, he'll be under your spell almost immediately. Remember when I went to Europe with those Frenchmen last year? I had them under my spell in less than five seconds of singing."

"Wow."

"Exactly."

Out of the corner of my eye, I see Natalie approaching. I tell Grandma Perkins, "Oh, gotta go. Ciao!" and then hang up.

"Who was that?" Natalie wants to know.

"My grandma."

She gives me a weird look. "I know she's cool and everything, but what's the deal? It's like you two are best buddies all of a sudden."

"Yeah, it's pretty bizarre," I agree, dropping my cell into my purse. "But I think she's just lonely or something."

Natalie snorts. "Grandma Perkins, *lonely*? I don't think so!"

I just laugh, but I know what she's getting at—and it bothers me. Of course, Natalie's not the only one who thinks Grandma's a bit of a slut. My parents do—not that they've ever said it outright, but I can just tell. And I used to think that too. But now, well, I'm thinking we might have it all wrong.

I stand up and Natalie follows me into the bathroom. After I've done my thing and am washing my hands, Natalie says, "So, I handed the waiter my Visa, and he just shook his head and said it was on the house. Whatever that means."

"It means it was free."

"No, I mean, *why* was it free?"

"Oh, yeah. I think the manager said something about being the ten-thousandth customer, so it's the big prize," I try, hoping she'll buy it.

I can all but see the little cogs turning in my best friend's head as she refreshes her lipstick. But she doesn't question it.

A young woman and a toddler emerge from the handicapped stall and commandeer the sinks. Natalie and I jump back so we won't get splashed.

"Well, thanks again for my dinner. Just because it was free doesn't mean it doesn't count." I hug her.

"You're quite welcome, Roxy. And your birthday celebration night is just beginning."

Before we leave, I practice making a coy Marilyn Monroe face in the mirror. Oh, how fun! I hope I can look like this next time I put somebody under my Siren spell.

Six

When Odysseus sailed past Anthemoessa Island unharmed, the three lovely Sirens flung themselves into the ferocious, unforgiving ocean, as the oracle had decreed.

"Um, Natalie? This isn't the way to the theater."

She brakes at a red light and looks over at me, a mysterious smile on her freshly lip-sticked mouth. "I know. We've had a change of plans."

"What do you mean? Where are we going?"

"To a party." She turns down her stereo, muffling Kelly Clarkson.

"*Whose* party?"

"J.T. Brewer's."

I shake my head, my mouth going dry. "No way, Natalie. Are you crazy? It's going to be a total Proud Crowd party. We're so not invited."

"*Au contraire, madame*," Natalie says in a faux French accent. "J.T. himself invited you."

I scrunch my nose and give her a look that clearly says, "How the heck did *you* know?"

"Alex told me. And it's a well-known fact that the invitation extends to all the friends of the invitee." The light turns green and she steps on the gas. "That's what makes it a *party*."

I slap my forehead. "Remember the last Proud Crowd party we went to?"

"What are you talking about?"

"Are you telling me you don't remember? You have no recollection of calling me last summer, begging me to go to Devin's house for a party? We weren't even invited; you just happened to overhear the jocks talking about it at Seven-Eleven. We bought new outfits and did each other's hair all cute and showed up right on time. Right on time to be left with Devin's bratty little brothers. We babysat them so the jocks could go to the *real* party, at Amber's house."

Natalie squeezes her steering wheel extra hard as she turns up University Boulevard. "Okay, okay. I remember. But Devin's parents paid us each five bucks an hour, and we snuck a wine cooler out of the fridge, so it wasn't *all* bad. Plus, that was a long time ago. We've all grown up a lot since then."

I cross my arms over my chest, still shocked to feel my new boobs. "Whatever."

A few moments later Natalie says, "Listen, Rox. *Everyone's* going to be there."

"So Alex is going? And what about Fuchsia, Ginny, Carl . . . and that new guy from Texas who plays the trumpet?"

"I know what you're thinking, Rox. We are *not* band geeks," she says indignantly. "We are talented musicians."

I really, *really* don't want to go to this party. I can't face the jocks. Not after the Zach's Date Incident. We're just a block or two from J.T.'s house, and I definitely have cold feet.

"Don't you want everyone to see you

after your makeover?" Natalie asks. "I'm serious. You look even better than Tess McGill in *Working Girl* or Allison Reynolds after Claire gets ahold of her in *The Breakfast Club*."

"When are you going to move on from all those eighties movies, Natalie?"

"You've got to respect the classics. But the point is, you look fabulous and Zach's going to go gaga over you."

Well, she's right about me looking fabulous. But could she be right about Zach? If I show up at this party, will I finally get that kiss I've been longing for? Yesterday, when I was an ordinary-looking BeeGee, doubtful. But now that I'm a Siren, is it possible?

Natalie gets a gleam in her eye as she says, "You know what? When I was at Seven-Eleven yesterday, I heard that Zach Parker and Eva the Diva are the newest residents of Splitsville."

"I never even knew they were back together. Didn't they break up at prom because he forgot to pick her up and she arrived fashionably late, and they crowned Amber Prom Princess in her place?"

"He didn't forget to pick her up, it's just that he forgot to pick her up in his uncle's

Bentley. So when he showed up in his pickup, she refused to get in. Anyway, they got back together that very night. And from what I hear, they did a whole lot more than just kiss and make up."

I forgot to mention another very important requisite of being in the Proud Crowd. Being a gossip. Obviously, Natalie's got that one down pat. "I know you fill up at Seven-Eleven just to get the latest scoop. Seriously, Natalie. You should start your own website."

"I'm just well-informed, that's all." She flicks some gum into her mouth and hands me a piece. "Point is, Zach's back in the game. And you, my dear, are gonna score."

An assortment of shiny SUVs are parked haphazardly up and down the steep, tree-lined street. I roll my window down, flooding Natalie's Sportage with the thumping of bass from J.T.'s Tudor-style house.

"Do you hear how loud the music is? The cops are going to be here any second," I say, rooting in my purse for lip gloss.

She parallel parks with the expertise of someone who's been driving for eight whole months and snorts. "Don't be such a sissy."

She hops out, and I pretend to be checking myself out in the visor mirror. But really, I'm putting my flute together and stuffing it down my shirt. I know Natalie would never let me get away with taking my whole flute case into a party. I might need it, though. Hopefully, no one will notice it if I tuck it down my cleavage and maneuver it down the front of my leg like this.

Acting against every fiber of my being, I follow her down the sidewalk, maneuvering the tip of my flute down the front of my pants as discreetly as possible. "Why do you even want to go to this party?" I ask. "Are you sick of the friends you already have?"

"I love my friends." She waits for me to catch up and then puts her arm around my shoulders. "Especially you. I'm *helping* you, Roxy. You want Zach, right? I'd bet my new Stella McCartney A-line miniskirt that he'll take notice of you tonight. I mean, look at you!" A huge smile spreads across her face.

It takes every ounce of self-control to keep from breaking into a smile myself. "You're so full of it. You were planning on dragging me to this party before you saw me as . . . um, someone who got a really great makeover." I clear my throat and do a little wiggle to shift my flute back in place.

She shrugs. "Maybe. But I knew you'd look cute regardless. And if you want Zach Parker, you've gotta meet him on his own turf. You know, let him see you hobnobbing with his circle of friends."

I know Natalie genuinely wants to help me, and there's probably a grain of truth in what she said about getting Zach to see me somewhere besides school. But the fact that Natalie wants more than anything to be a Franklin High A-lister isn't lost on me.

"Okay, but when I want to leave, you have to promise to take me home," I say as we cross through J.T's front yard. "It's my birthday, you know."

Crap. This flute-down-the-shirt thing isn't exactly comfortable. Can people see it? Note to self: No hugging and no slow dancing with anybody.

She raises her delicate eyebrow. "Deal."

We slip through the front door, Eminem's music giving me an insta-headache. About twenty teenagers are jammed into the living room—some dancing, some lounging on the white leather couches. Everyone's shouting, and it reeks of sweat and cologne and beer. This must've been what Kurt Cobain meant by "Smells Like Teen Spirit."

"Do you see him?" I ask.

Natalie shakes her head.

We wander over to the fireplace to get a better look. By now, more and more partiers are taking notice of us, and there's a lot of whispering going on. I strain to hear what they're saying, but it's too loud in here.

"Let's get a drink," Natalie yells over the music, grabbing my hand. She yanks me past the gyrating sea of bodies to the kitchen, where one of the Proud Crowd chicks is doing a keg stand, the hem of her skirt sliding down to expose her pastel yellow panties.

"Fourteen . . . fifteen . . . sixteen . . . ," the mob chants.

The guys promptly stop counting when they see us, and a cheerleader performs a bubbly solo from back by the dishwasher. Her voice trails off after "twenty-one." The chick on the keg spits the tap out, a stream of beer squirting out.

Every guy in the room stares at me, mouth agog.

I snatch the tap away from the dazed keg master (who is still spraying people with beer) and pass it to Natalie. "I'm going to go outside for a sec. I just need some fresh air," I tell her, my flute painfully poking into my thigh.

"Okay, hang on." She passes me a flimsy white plastic cup half full of lukewarm beer, half full of foam. I escape out the back door. I'm excited for Zach to see me like this, but I'm pretty nervous too. I'm not quite ready to "bump into" him. I need to collect my thoughts, psych myself up.

There's an old swing set by the back fence, creaking lazily in the evening breeze. I walk over to it and try to sit on the swing, but I'm not bending very well with this flute down my shirt. So I just lean against the pole and raise the beer to my lips. I take one sip and spit it out. Disgusting. Especially mixed with spearmint gum. I spit the gum out and it ricochets off the fence.

Rustling noises are coming from behind the garage. Probably just a couple getting it on. Too bad Natalie's not here to quench her gossip thirst. I hear a voice that sounds an awful lot like Devin's. "I wonder if Zach's nerdy little date is gonna make it," he says, not very quietly.

Oh my God. Are they talking about *me*? I tiptoe closer to the garage, trying to keep my flip-flops from click-clacking on my heels.

"Dude, she's not all that bad." Is that Zach? "There's something . . . about her. About the way she's always staring at me and pretending not to."

Devin says, "Shit, dude. No more beer for you. She's a BeeGee, for Chrissake."

Now J.T. is talking. "I know what Zach means. Band geeks can be hot. Maybe she does that flute thing like that chick in that movie."

Oh, yeah. Like *that's* original. We flutists will never live that down, thank-you-very-much, *American Pie*.

"Shit, dude," Zach and Devin groan in unison.

Then Devin says, "Hell, Zachster. You've got Eva wrapped around your little finger. No BeeGee in the world would make me give up *that* fine booty."

"Yeah," J.T. says, laughing. "No matter how many times she did the band camp flute act for your viewing pleasure."

Without warning, the jocks wander out from behind the garage and immediately spot me. My wrist goes slack and then I freeze, beer spilling on my feet, heart banging hard against my flute.

Seven

Though Leucosia's beautiful body was discovered washed up on the shores of Southern Italy, her sisters Pisinoe and Thelxiepia swam to the safety of a nearby island. The ruthless sea had battered Pisinoe's body, and she knew her days were few.

"Hello?" Zach finally says, a strange look on his face.

The other two are looking me up and down, down and up. Great. They probably see the flute bulge.

"For-*get* Eva," Devin says under his breath.

"Who are you?" J.T. asks.

Why am I so surprised they don't recognize me? I mean, my own father didn't recognize me.

"I'm . . . a talented musician." Oh God, can I be any lamer?

Zach's mouth—the very mouth I was dying to kiss only yesterday—is hanging open as wide as that *Scream* dude's. "Roxy?"

I've got to get out of here before I completely shatter this whole Siren vibe. Scurrying away in the overgrown grass as fast as possible in my flip-flops, I burst through the back door. I scan the kitchen, but Natalie's AWOL.

"Have you seen Natalie O'Brien?" I ask no one in particular.

"Who?"

"Who's she looking for?"

"Natalie O'Brien," I repeat, louder.

"Never heard of her."

I say, "She was the keg mistress only minutes ago." Everybody stares back cluelessly. "Pretty girl, dark brown flippy hair. Wearing a black sundress . . . ?" Nothing. This must be what it's like to play charades with a bunch of blind people.

Oh, God. Don't make me say it. Please don't make me do this. Ever so quietly, I whisper, "She plays flute . . . in the band?"

Someone laughs, and more people join in. "A band geek?"

"There aren't any BeeGees here."

"Hell, no!"

"As if!"

"Hey, we just kicked one out. Maybe it was her."

Then I catch sight of Natalie, standing by the bay window with . . . a dude in a short-sleeved plaid shirt, long camo cargo shorts, and Converse high-tops. Alex?

I can't believe he's here. Did he come by himself? I've watched enough movies to know he's asking for trouble. It's like an unwritten rule that if you're a) uninvited and b) a *guy*, you may as well duck, 'cause you're about to get slugged by someone who lifts weights at least three times a week.

Devin follows my gaze and yells, "What is this? Band practice? Who invited *them*?"

Who turned off the music? I wonder.

A girl with a diamond stud in her nose taps me on the shoulder. "Hey, is that the chick you're looking for?" she asks.

Natalie shoots me a wide-eyed let's-get-outta-here look from across the room.

I take a step toward my friends and then

stop. Zach is standing right beside me, and he's smiling at me. At *me*!

I feel like I'm in a gigantic taffy machine—being pulled in every possible direction. I'm surrounded by hard biceps, tanned skin, perfect teeth, great butts (one in particular) . . .

"You're at the wrong party, dude," J.T. yells at Alex. I'm sure Alex heard him, but his expression stays neutral.

"We already kicked your girlfriend out," the guy standing right behind me shouts. "But on second thought, she can stay. I hear she gives great—"

I stomp on the guy's foot as hard as I can, but he just laughs and slaps J.T. a high-five.

Natalie's meticulously made-up eyes tear up, and Alex leads her through a group of gawking partiers. Before I know it, the door bangs, and Natalie and Alex are gone.

I take a few steps toward the front door, but Darren Smith, Franklin High's up-and-coming senior class president, gets in my face and professes his undying love for me. His smells of beer and Axe bodyspray. "You're the most *gor*-geous lady I ever laid eyes on. Please take this as a token of my love," he slurs, holding out a wine cooler. Oh my God. How embarrassing! I take the bottle, mainly just to shut him up.

I feel like I've just gotten off the teacups ride at Disney World. All the partiers are spinning around the room, closing in on me. Making it impossible to breathe.

Where'd Zach go?

I dash down the hall (as quick as I can with a flute down my shirt) and bust through a bedroom door. It's dark and musky-smelling. I flip on the light switch. There's a guy and a girl on the bed doing something I really wish I didn't just see.

"Oh, God. Sorry! I'll just get out of your way . . . I'll just go." I slam the door shut— and then remember I left the light on. I open the door again, flip off the light, and scuttle down the hallway to another room.

This one's dark and chilly and (thank God) empty. There's a queen-size brass bed on one end and an armoire on the other. It's a pretty, frilly room, probably for guests. I head over to the window. Sheer white curtains flutter in a waft of AC. I pull them back and look for my friends. They're nowhere in sight.

I should just go home. Zach obviously found something more exciting to do than hang out with me. And the sooner I leave, the sooner I can take this freaking flute out. I'm probably getting a rash or something.

"Roxy?" Zach's six foot, three inch frame is blocking the doorway. My heart skips a beat. God, he's gorgeous. "Don't take this the wrong way, but were you always this hot?" he asks me.

The only sound I can make is a weird snort-laugh.

"You're beautiful. I can't stop staring at you. It's like you've got some kind of power over me," Zach says, reaching for my shaking hand.

Oh my God. I can't believe this is happening. I look down at our hands. It's all so surreal. He's *touching* me. I'm in a bedroom with the hottest guy at Franklin and he's telling me that I'm beautiful.

He must be wasted. "You're drunk, Zach."

He shakes his head. "Nope, but J.T.'s completely sloshed. Another beer or two and we're going to shave his unibrow."

I crack up.

Zach bends his elbow, bringing me into his chest like a dance move. I step back, hoping he didn't feel the flute. Oooh, that smile.

"What's that?" He reaches out and touches my flute, right below my boob.

"It's my flute." Kill me now.

He raises an eyebrow. "You couldn't leave it at home?"

"Well, I *could*, I guess, but it would get all freaked out and piddle on the rug."

Zach chuckles, and I think I just might be in heaven.

Until Eva breezes into the room in her beaded sandals with the three-inch heels, completely shattering the whole heaven vibe. I mean, they don't allow the devil in heaven, do they? "Hey, sorry I'm late. I've had the worst night ever. My flatiron decided to die on me so I had to go over to Amber's and . . ." She stops talking, apparently noticing me for the first time. She sizes me up, squinting her left eye. Then she practically growls, "Who are you?" She's so close I can smell her shampoo. I don't know what kind it is, but it smells a lot better than the Suave I use.

"It's Roxy, from school," Zach says, grinning.

Amber sidles up to Eva. I was wondering what was taking her so long. "Wow, you look amazing!" Amber says to me.

"Where'd you get your hair done?"

Eva steps in front of Amber. She raises one of her eyebrows, giving her the appearance of someone deep in thought. "Ah, yes. I remember you. You're the one who's always staring at Zach."

Amber giggles and I take a deep breath. Time to play nice. "I like your dress, Eva. It's Marc Jacobs, right?" Normally, I wouldn't know the difference between Marc Jacobs and Old Navy. But Natalie saw Eva buying it at Nordstrom, and this dress matches Natalie's description to a T. I'm always learning what's in just by hanging with Natalie, via osmosis or something.

Eva taps her French-manicured fingers on her cheek. "Oh my God. Amber, did you hear that? The band geek knows something about fashion. Who would've thought?"

Amber laughs loudly, as cheerleaders do, and my blood boils. "It must've cost a fortune," I say between clenched teeth. No more Miss Nice Siren.

"My mother's a prominent plastic surgeon, you know. I can afford it."

"It's such a shame there's berry wine cooler all over it. I'm sure it's *ruined*."

Eva's supershiny lips part and she looks

down at her cream-colored dress. "There's not—" At that very instant, I pour the entire wine cooler down her front.

"You *bitch*!" she screams, seething.

Oh my God! Now what? I wish there were a TelePrompTer in here—something to give me my next line. I turn on my heels and dash for the front door, my flute jabbing into my stomach and thigh with every step.

Zach runs after me out into the yard, leaving the screaming girls in the dust. "Roxy, hold up!"

All right, Roxy. Time to show Zach Parker that a Siren is a force to be reckoned with. I stop and turn around. "Is that why you keep in such good shape? So you can chase girls?" I ask, my hands on my hips. This feels so weird, flirting with Zach Parker. But I can do so much better than just flirt, can't I?

I reach between my boobs and slowly pull out my flute. His light blue eyes grow bigger and bigger. Ahhh. Much better. Note to self: Never stash flute in shirt again. Overall awkwardness score: eleven out of ten.

By the time I start playing, Zach is grinning from ear to ear. I play a few more notes, for good measure, and give him the Marilyn Monroe look.

A gust of wind whips past, and I can feel my long, smooth, beautiful hair floating up around my head. I curl my finger and he comes so close I can smell his Polo cologne and a slight hint of Fritos on his breath.

"I'd like you to ask me out for tomorrow night," I whisper in my best Siren voice.

He nods. "Do you wanna go out tomorrow night?"

Oh, joy. Eva, Amber, J.T., and Devin are standing on the front stoop, gawking. How long have they been there?

Devin says, "Dude, did she just pull a flute out of her—"

"Zach?" Eva interrupts, storming over to us. "Did I hear you ask her out?"

Zach nods, still looking at me.

Amber says, "You and Zach aren't together anymore, remember?" and I swear steam comes out of from Eva's ears. Amber slaps her hand over her mouth and "Oh, God! Sorry, sorry, sorry!" leaks out between her fingers.

Eva snatches my flute and waves it around, the moonlight reflecting off of it. "What's this? You bring your . . . *instrument* to parties? Parties, I might point out, that you're not even *invited* to?"

My face is on fire. "Actually, I *was* invited. But it doesn't matter, because I was just leaving."

Eva fixes me with her subzero stare. "Well, don't forget this." She shoves my flute in my face and I grab it from her. "Bye-bye Roxy. See ya this fall at football games. I'm sure you'll be looking extra glamorous in your big fuzzy hat, marching around the field at halftime."

Amber laughs hysterically, and when she realizes she's the only one laughing, shrugs. "Well. The party's inside, so, uh, let's go." The Proud Crowd parades through the front door, all but Eva and Zach.

Eva grabs Zach by the collar and pulls him down to her level, gazing at him through her eyelashes. "I know we just broke up, but I'm ready to do a little makin' up. How about we go somewhere a little more . . . intimate?"

"Why?" he asks.

Not so subtly, she rubs against him. "You *know* why."

Zach gently pushes her away, and I've never seen Eva the Diva look so mad. Is this how she looked when Amber got crowned Prom Princess? Man, I would've loved to see that, but I had a bad case of No Date–itis. Grasping my flute, I smile to myself. I have a feeling Roxy Zimmerman will be going to next year's prom, no problem.

Eva storms back into the house and slams the door, the brass knocker clanking in response.

"So what do you say, Roxy? Wanna go out tomorrow night?"

Aaaaaaah!

"Sure," I say. Which is code for "Of *course* I do, you idiot!"

Too bad Natalie isn't here. She'd be so proud!

But Natalie's Sportage is long gone. There's just an empty space where it had been parked. Should I have left when she and Alex did? God, everything happened so fast. Have I made a huge mistake, staying at this party?

I look up at the midnight blue sky. Beyond the wispy clouds, the moon shines bright and silvery. Stars twinkle like crazy. It's like when Chase flips the lights on and off as fast as he can, just to annoy me.

"Roxy? You all right?" Zach asks.

"Um, yeah. I'm just tired." I pull out my cell phone.

"Who're you calling?" He stuffs his hands in his jeans pockets, looking über-adorable.

"I'm just calling—" But wait. If I ask my parents for a ride, they'll want to know why Natalie isn't taking me home. And I don't particularly feel like explaining it to them. "Nobody. Um, just checking to see if . . . I have any text messages," I lie.

What if *Zach Parker* drove me home? Oh man, I'm getting goosebumps just thinking about it. I bite my lower lip and conjure up the courage to ask, "Can you take me home?"

"Sure."

Inside, I'm screaming and jumping up and down, but on the outside, I'm just looking at him in what I hope is a superconfident I-knew-you'd-say-yes way. I follow Zach to his truck, which is parked in the driveway, and I can't help but wonder if (and hope that) we've got an audience.

He says, "It's open," and I hop in. In the few seconds that the interior light comes on, I see that the gray upholstery is dingy and sunflower seed shells are scattered all over the floor. An empty twenty-ounce bottle of Mountain Dew is tucked into the cup holder and there's a nasty crack in the windshield.

He blasts his Green Day CD and drums his steering wheel as if he's Tré Cool. Too bad he's not in band. He could actually learn a thing or two about rhythm. We go a few miles like this before I say (or shout, more like, seeing as how he's got his stereo on so freaking loud), "Thanks for taking me home." He's got one of those CD holders on the passenger side visor, and it's so over-stuffed, the visor keeps inching its way into the down position.

"Huh?"

He's not taking the hint, so I reach over and turn the volume down myself. "Thanks for driving me home."

The only other conversation we have the rest of the way is me rattling off directions, since he's obviously never been to my house. I swear, I could find my way to his house blindfolded. Ha. Not like I'd ever tell him that. He'd think I was a stalker or something. Am I?

His truck grunts and moans its way up my driveway, the headlights illuminating the marigolds and pansies ringing the mailbox post. The porch light makes the front door seem more purple than red. Judging by the muted glow coming from my bedroom window, Mom must've turned on my bedside lamp for me.

This is all so crazy. I mean, I'm actually sitting in Zach Parker's truck. With Zach Parker!

His arm stretches out across my shoulders, knocking my tank top strap down. Here I am, gazing into his baby blue eyes, not knowing what to do, what to say, what to think. I tug my strap back in place and bite my lower lip. Zach is frozen like a cherry Slurpee. It's as if he's waiting for some kind of sign.

This is it. This is my chance to kiss Zach Parker, right here in his white Toyota pickup. But what if he pulls away? What if he laughs at me or calls me Peppermint Patty? I take a deep breath: *iiiiin, ouuuuut*. If I jump out of his truck right this very instant, I won't sink any further into the humiliation quicksand. But if I go for it . . . I might actually be pulled out of the quicksand completely.

I steal a look at myself in his side mirror. I'm not the frizzy-haired, zit-faced band geek I was yesterday. I'm a beautiful Siren.

Any guy would give his sports scholarship to make out with me. (I know that sounds conceited, but I'm totally nervous and maybe if I psych myself up, I'll actually have the guts to try to get that kiss I've been dreaming about all these years.)

Go for it, Roxy.

"Kiss me," I hear myself whisper.

"Yeah?"

I nod, hoping it's dark enough to hide the blush I feel creeping into my cheeks. "Yeah."

Zach inhales deeply and cradles the back of my head. Oh my God, it's really happening. I close my eyes and wait, my lips tingling in anticipation. I feel his breath on my nose as he exhales. . . . Oh, here it comes!

Or maybe not.

Hey, what's taking him so long?

What's wrong? Oh my God. Is there something in my nose? Is my lip gloss smeared on my teeth? Is it my breath? Has he changed his mind? Has the Siren spell expired?

Opening my right eye just the teensiest bit, I peep at him through my lashes. He's just sitting there, staring at me. There's a serious expression on his face, but he doesn't look particularly repulsed, so that's good. He leans closer, and I close my eyes again, my heart beating in overdrive.

Zach's lips hit mine, his tongue banging against my teeth until I open up. He swipes his tongue side-to-side, front-to-back. Wet, hard, hot. And did I mention *wet*?

I yank my head away, pressing my fingers against my throbbing, slobbery lips. I've been waiting for this moment since puberty. My first real kiss. Not a forehead kiss like my mom gives me, or a cheek kiss like Alex and Natalie give me. Not a kiss mandated by those dumb kissing games we'd play at camp. A Real Kiss.

Is this how it's *supposed* to feel? If fireworks were supposed to go off, someone forgot to light them. Hell, they forgot to go to the neighborhood TNT shed and buy them in the first place. I feel no tingles, no sparks, no excitement. Instead, I'm rehearsing some kind of excuse to get out of his tube socks–stinky truck and into the safety of my home.

I open the door and the interior lights come on. Something sparkly catches my eye. Reaching into the crack between the seat belt and the seat, I pull out a pretty rhinestone hair clip. Eva Nelson's hair clip. She wears it all the time. I would too, if it were mine. Well, she won't ever see it again if I leave it in this mess of a vehicle, right? I slip it into my pocket, making a mental note to give it back to her the next time I see her.

"See ya later," I say, jumping out.

Right before I slip inside the front door, I hear Zach shout, "Hey, you forgot your flute!"

"Oh, right . . . thanks."

Eight

I slip inside and close the door as quietly as possible, but Pumpkin hears me and comes a-prancin' over, his tail wagging enthusiastically. Leaning aginst the door, I clench my eyes shut and try to catch my breath.

What an unbelievable night! First, I can't believe I showed my face at a Proud Crowd party, especially after Eva and J.T. teased me about liking Zach. Second, I can't believe I actually kissed Zach Parker. Definitely not the toe-curling kind of kiss you see in the movies, but it was a kiss. And any kiss is better than no kiss, right?

Besides, it was probably my fault that it wasn't all that. I mean, Zach has tons of experience. He was with Eva, after all. And she's not exactly the president of the Prudence Club. I, on the other hand, have zero experience. Maybe it'll just take a little more practice to get it right.

I've got to call Natalie to dish. After dropping my flute off in my room, I dial her number into my cordless, and wait for her to answer. Pumpkin yawns, showing me a mouthful of teensy white teeth and a teensy pink tongue. I stoop down and scratch his ears.

"It's one thing to be a bitch to *me*, but to Alex?" she says, skipping the "hello" altogether.

"What are you talking about?" I wander into the kitchen and pour myself a glass of milk.

"You totally dissed us."

"Excuse me? *You're* the one who dissed *me*. I had to find a ride home." I sit down with a slice of leftover birthday cake.

"I guess you think you're all of a sudden too *pretty* to be seen with the likes of me." She says "pretty" all nasally, like it's a bad thing.

"Whatever, Natalie," I say with my mouth full of cream-cheese frosting. But part of me knows she's right. I had a feeling those guys wouldn't kick me out, like they did Natalie and Alex. I knew, deep down, that my Siren beauty was enough to earn me at least a temporary Proud Crowd membership card. I admit it. And I can't deny that I took advantage of this once-in-a-lifetime opportunity to hang out with them, even for a jiffy. I'm not necessarily proud of this, and if life had a rewind button, I probably would've left with Natalie and Alex.

Then again, if I'd left, I wouldn't have kissed Zach.

Still, I don't want Natalie to be mad at me. I know what will bring her around. Just the mere mention of The Kiss . . . "Hey, guess what?"

"I've gotta go."

"Don't you want to know what happened?"

"I *saw* what happened, Roxy. I may not have perfect eyesight like you in your new colored contacts, but I saw what happened." She pauses for a second before continuing. "You sold me out, Roxy. You sold Alex and me out. You made fun of us for being band geeks, and you pretended not to even know us. It may as well have been *you* who kicked us out of the party."

The bite of cake lodges itself in my throat. I take a swig of milk to wash it down. "That's so untrue! Why would I make fun of band geeks when I'm one myself?"

"You tell me."

"I'm serious, Natalie. You're being ridiculous."

"Am I? Then why'd you stay? Why'd you stay when they were being such jerks? I thought you were my best friend, Roxy. Friends stick together. They stick up for you! They don't humiliate you in front of the whole damn world. They don't pretend not to even *know* you."

Her words make my stomach plummet, like I'm on the Tower of Terror ride at MGM Studios. "Natalie, I . . ." Man, I figured she wouldn't be happy with me, but I had no clue she'd be *this* upset. I need to give her time to let off some steam, so I change the subject back to the whole reason we even went to the party. "You don't care who drove me home in his white Toyota pickup?" Come on. Be a good little gossip hound and take this bone. This big meaty, delicious bone.

She says, "Not really," and the line goes dead.

I brush my teeth and climb into bed, my breaths coming in quick, shallow waves. Snuggled under my daisy comforter with Pumpkin snoring softly at my feet, I stew over Natalie.

I didn't expect her to be this mad about the whole staying-at-the-party thing. But wasn't the reason Natalie dragged me to the party so that Zach could see the "new me" somewhere other than at school? Didn't she want him to ask me out? Didn't she want him to kiss me?

As for The Kiss, well, I'm going to have to do something about that. Maybe if I use my Siren powers on Zach again, I can get him to kiss me like the hero in one of those romance novels Mom has stashed under her bed—you know, the ones with muscle-ripped, half-naked men holding huge-breasted women on the cover?

While I'm eating breakfast Sunday morning, I have an idea. An epiphany, really. I am a Siren. I have powers. Why do all my tedious household chores myself when I've got a perfectly competent little brother with nothing better to do?

I pull out my flute, and the instant

Chase comes wandering into the kitchen, I start playing. Beautiful, smooth, sweet music fills the air. I play for quite a while, since a) he's not already under the spell of my beauty (he *is* my brother, after all) and b) I haven't played my flute for him since becoming a Siren.

Chase smiles this goofy smile and lays his beloved Game Boy on the counter.

Oh my God, it's working. This is too cool!

Without warning, he hurls a banana at me. The banana ricochets off the top of my head and knocks over my glass of SunnyD. I spring up before the orange stickiness drenches my pajama pants, and Chase takes off into the dining room. Grabbing my flute, I run after him, blowing notes into it as I chase him around the house.

I'm about to give up when strangest thing happens. My brother stops running and walks back into the kitchen. His pupils are dilated as if he just got back from the eye doctor.

I give the whole Siren power thing another whirl. "Chase, I'd like you to do the dishes, wash and iron all my dirty clothes, clean my room and bathroom, and feed Pumpkin. All summer long." I get ready to duck for another banana-bomb, but since he's just standing there looking at me, I add as an afterthought, "And get a haircut. You look ridiculous."

He blinks once, twice . . . then says, "You betcha, Roxy. Anything else I can do for you?"

"Er, no. That'll be all." *Hello?* This is my little brother we're talking about. True to his word, he whisks away my cereal bowl and empty glass and takes them to the sink.

I run my fingers along my beat-up flute case, marveling at the shiny, silver power within it. Funny how the very thing that's been the bane of my existence since the fifth grade is capable of giving me any kind of life I want. Like Grandma Perkins said, the sky's the limit.

As I'm hunting through my closet for something to wear, Chase zips about— making my bed, vacuuming my carpet, and even washing my bedroom window.

Examining myself in the mirror, I still have a hard time believing this is my reflection. All my life, I've dreamed of being beautiful. But I never dreamed that it would actually come true. And I never dreamed that I'd be going out with the hottest guy at Franklin!

The phone rings, and Chase lunges for it. "Hello? Yeah, she's here. Just a sec." He holds the phone out for me, and before I can wonder who it is, he says, "It's a booooooy."

I snatch the phone, feeling the heat in my cheeks. "Hello?"

"Hi, Roxy! It's me, Zach. I'm calling about tonight. Are we still on?" Chase is doing that sick thing where he folds his eyelids up. I wish they'd stick like that.

"Zach? Hang on, 'kay?"

I throw the phone down on my bed and shove Chase out of my room.

"But I'm not done cleaning!" he cries through the door.

"You can finish later," I hiss back at him.

I run back to the phone and pick it up. Zach Parker is on my phone. Zach Parker called me. We're going out tonight!

"Hello? Roxy, you there? I can hear you breathing."

"Oh, yeah." God, how embarrassing. "I'm back. Sorry about that."

"So, do you want me to come get you around seven?"

"Yes."

After a pause, he says, "Okay. See you then."

I hang up the phone, throw myself on my freshly made bed, and scream.

Chase bangs on my door. "Roxy! Hurry, let me in. I've still gotta dust."

While Mom pops a Tupperware full of left-over Chinese food into the microwave, I pour myself a glass of water. "Chase has been begging me to take him to get his hair cut," she says. "So if you want, you can come with us and we can hit Cold Stone for some ice cream afterward."

"That sounds fun, Mom . . ." Not really, but I don't want to hurt her feelings. "But unfortunately, I've got plans."

"Oh? With Natalie?"

"Uh, no. Zach Parker, actually." I wait for it to register that Franklin High's hottest hottie and star quarterback is about to pick up her very own flesh-and-blood daughter.

"You've never mentioned him before. Does he go to your school?" She presses a bunch of buttons on the microwave and nukes away. "Whatever happened to Alex?"

"What do you mean?"

"Alex McCoy, that nice boy who plays the trombone. Weren't you two going with each other?"

"Going where?"

"You know, going steady. I could've sworn——"

I roll my eyes. "Mom, we're just friends," and she gives me this weird look, so I add, "He's in *band* with me."

"I see."

I pick a piece of lint off my newest Roxy shirt, marveling at how good it looks now that I've got boobs. Right as the microwave buzzes, the doorbell rings and I rush to answer it before Chase.

Zach stands on the welcome mat, his hands stuffed deep into his jeans pockets. His hair's combed and he's wearing a faded American Eagle polo. "You look great, Roxy. Really rockin'."

"Thanks. You too." I grab my purse (holding my flute, which, thank goodness, breaks down into three pieces) and follow him to his truck. I'm going on a *date* with Zach Parker. Somebody pinch me! No, wait. If I'm dreaming, I never want to wake up.

Dad whips up the driveway in his red

Boxster and waves, doing a double take when he sees that I'm with a boy. Waving back at him, I hurry and jump into Zach's truck before Dad can say anything to embarrass me.

"Wow, your pop has a sweet ride," Zach says. "Do you ever get to take it?"

"No. It's like his pride and joy. He doesn't even let Mom drive it."

"Bummer. So, what's the plan tonight?" Zach asks, reversing down the driveway.

Plan, right. I guess I never really thought about *what* we're going to do tonight. Is it like totally old-fashioned to expect *him* to have an itinerary? After all, he's the one who asked me out. Okay, technically, I used my Siren powers to get him to ask me out. Back to square one. "I don't know. What do you think?" I ask, clearing away some space for my feet among all the trash in his truck. Now the bottoms of my flip-flops are totally sticky. The culprit: lemon-lime Gatorade that's spilled all over the floor.

"I don't care."

"We could go to that new Orlando Bloom movie," I throw out.

"Okay."

I almost laugh. Is he for real? Did he just freely offer to go to a chick flick without kicking, screaming, crying, or making me sign an "I Promise to Put Out" agreement? Couldn't this get him excommunicated from the Church of Dude?

"Mind if I play something?" I ask, pulling my flute out of my purse and twisting the parts together.

His forehead furrows, but he says, "Knock yourself out," and turns off his Green Day CD.

My heart is palpitating like crazy. The last thing I want to do is to spotlight my band geekiness. But if Zach and I are going to do the dating thing, I may as well have happy lips, right? Why wait around for "Practice makes perfect" when I'm a Siren?

After playing my song, I ask Zach to pull over in the Chuck E. Cheese's parking lot, and he does. I swear his pupils are eclipsing his irises. He looks like one of those Japanese cartoon characters. "Kiss me again. But this time, more like a hero out of a romance novel."

"Come again?"

Right. He's probably never read one, or even skimmed one for the naughty parts like Natalie and I used to do. Stupid me. "Er, like Enrique Iglesias?" I try. "You know, the way he kissed Anna Kournikova in the 'Escape' video? You do watch MTV, don't you? It was voted one of the sexiest videos in hist—"

Before I can babble another word, he pulls me close and gently nibbles my lower lip. Oh, wow. Next, his lips skirt mine playfully, teasing me. And for the grand finale, we come together in a kiss so fiery and passionate, I don't want it to ever end. *Mmmmmmmm.*

After we finally break apart, chests heaving, he leans back in his seat and utters a very eloquent, "Whoa."

Couldn't have said it better myself.

When Zach and I get to the movie theater, we stroll to the ticket booth hand in hand. I'm still a little woozy from The Kiss. And I guess that's why I don't notice Natalie in the opposite line. "What is this?" she almost shouts, hands on her designer-jeaned hips. "You're too cool to say hi to your best friend?"

Ginny, Carl, and Fuchsia wander over to us with their Red Vines and popcorn. I'm about to ask which movie they're all going to when Zach sticks his fingers in his mouth and whistles, nearly busting my eardrum.

"Yo, Zach!" Devin shouts, jogging over. J.T., Eva, and Amber—all dressed like Abercrombie & Fitch model wannabes—follow.

Eva flips her long blond hair. "Oh my God, Zach. Did you get hit in the head with a football or something? Why the hell are you out in public with *her*?"

Her question hangs in the butter-scented air as the Proud Crowd sneers and the BeeGees stare at their grubby sneakers. (Except for Natalie, of course, who's wearing the cutest wedge sandals.)

Eva takes a step closer to me and hisses, "Just because you're not ugly anymore doesn't mean you're one of us."

"She's a helluva lot hotter than you two put together," J.T. says to Eva and Amber.

It looks like fire is going to shoot out of Eva's eyes any second.

Instead of lashing out at the jocks, the cheerleaders swim around Natalie like chicly dressed sharks. Amber hisses, "You might have cute clothes, but that doesn't make *you* one of us, either."

"What*ever*," Eva says with a dismissive

flick of her hand. "She gets her whole wardrobe at the Castle Rock Outlets."

I say, "And how would you know?" but Zach snatches my arm and leads me down the hall before I can say anything else or hear Eva's response. I look over my shoulder at Natalie. She's making a face like she's in the midst of a Brazilian bikini wax. Tears glisten in the corners of her big blue eyes. But I know she won't cry. Not in front of the Proud Crowd.

I should've channeled Lara Croft and punched Eva and Amber's fake-tanned faces until they both needed nose jobs (which isn't quite as mean as it sounds 'cause Eva's mom is a plastic surgeon so they'd get their operations for free). I should've told Natalie that I'm sorry for staying at the party, that I'm sorry I pretended we weren't friends. I mean, she's still my best friend, right?

But she's already heading down the far hall, her Kate Spade knockoff bouncing against her skinny thigh. The Proud Crowd trails behind Zach and me and then veers off to the concession stand.

"Roxy?"

I whip around, suddenly face-to-face with Alex.

I'm totally shocked, but I manage to say, "Alex, hey."

"Hi." He grins at me, his cheeks flushed.

"So, you work here?" *Duh.* He wouldn't be standing here in a hideous blue-and-yellow-striped shirt and too-short black pants, taking our tickets just for kicks. "I mean, I thought you said you were working at the Auto Spa this summer," I recover.

Zach crosses in front of Alex and says to me, "I'm gonna go get some popcorn. Want any?"

"Yeah, thanks." Once Zach's out of earshot, I ask Alex, "Did you see Natalie and the gang?"

He nods. "Yeah, I saw all of you talking. So, you're coming with us to Murphy's, I take it?" he asks.

I try to shrug it off like it's no big deal, but it's strange that they're all going to Murphy's and no one even mentioned it. Of course, it's our favorite hangout and it's not like I need a special invitation. "Maybe."

"You look pretty, Rox. Your hair, your glasses . . . um, not that there was anything wrong with . . ." He stares down at his Converse high-tops.

I smile. "Thanks, Alex."

"Um, can I ask you something? Are you and Zach . . . ?"

As if on cue, Zach materializes beside me. "There you are. Ready?" He wraps his sinewy arm around my back, a huge tub of popcorn in his other hand.

"Yep." I wave to Alex and head down the hall with Zach. "You sure got that popcorn fast," I say, helping myself to a handful.

"Yeah, well, Eva was already in line, so she just got us some." Oh, joy. I guarantee she spat in it.

"Are your friends coming to this movie?" I ask during a trailer for a Jack Black movie that looks even funnier than the last one.

"Dunno." He shrugs. "Don't care."

I rest my head on Zach's shoulder and he combs his fingers through my hair, and it feels *fab*ulous.

Until it snags on his varsity ring. After a rather painful detangling, we start kissing. Before long, we're in the depths of a full-fledged make-out session. He gives me one nibbling, lip-skirting, fiery kiss after another until the credits roll.

As Zach is driving to my house after

the movie, part of me wants to drop by Murphy's. I'm sure he'd say yes, especially if I mention how good the fries are. Or if I put my flute to work. But the part of me that's scared how my friends will react to my showing up at our favorite hangout with Zach Parker ultimately wins out. Besides, all that making out has made me tired.

Zach pulls up my driveway and we unbuckle our seat belts. He snakes his arm over the back of the bench seat, his fingers twirling my hair. When we lean together to kiss, I'm happy to report it's perfect. Exactly like the kisses he's been giving me since the one in the Chuck E. Cheese's parking lot.

I float inside the house. The 'rents are staked out on the couch in the living room. Dad's watching *Star Wars* for the zillionth time. Mom's reading a paperback, her reading glasses propped haphazardly on her nose. She looks up when I come in and says, "Hello, dear. Did you have a nice night?"

"Uh-huh."

She removes her glasses and folds them on her lap. "Your father and I need to talk to you about something."

Uh-oh. Now what? I'm by no means the

perfect teenage daughter, but I'm not used to having my parents gang up on me like this. To be honest, I'm a little scared.

She swipes the remote control from Dad and pauses his movie. He clears his throat and says, "That's right, honey. Why don't you sit down?"

Slowly, I lower myself onto the blue leather recliner.

My parents exchange a look, and I'm guessing they're silently debating which one has to start this "talk."

Mom must've won. Or lost, depending on your point of view. She says, "Roxy, we don't know what you're holding over Chase's head . . . but it's going to stop. You can't make your brother do all your chores."

"He said no to Grayson's birthday party because he wasn't finished with your laundry," Dad adds, "and he's not keeping up with his own duties around the house."

Mom fingers the afghan that's draped on her armrest and then looks me in the eye. "Are you blackmailing him, Roxy?"

"Of course not!" I cross my arms over my chest. "I think he's just trying to be extra nice to me for some reason." By the look they give me, it's obvious they're not buying it. So I try, "I have no idea what is going on in that twelve-year old little boy mind of his. But I'll talk to him. I'll make sure he stops sacrificing his own chores and his social life to help me out. Okay?"

Mom sighs and hands Dad the remote. "Okay. So . . . what was the movie about?" she asks.

Crap. This lying is getting out of control. "Uh, Orlando Bloom plays this really hot guy who meets this girl and they fall in love and, uh, live happily ever after."

I have no clue what was happening on the big screen. I was in my own little world, the world where hot jocks go for band geeks and live happily ever after. But hey, it would've been nice to get a glimpse of Orlando's naked butt.

Nine

It's Monday and I'm sitting in the waiting room at the DMV on Colorado Boulevard. Mom had some kind of Junior League fundraiser thing and, of course, Dad had to work. Alex was nice enough to drive me here so I could take my test and get my driver's license.

The fluorescent lights flicker and buzz, and some chick's hammering her pencil on a pockmarked desk while she takes the written exam. Talk about annoying.

"Did you have fun last night?" Alex asks out of the blue.

"Yeah. It was a really good movie."

"Really? I haven't seen it yet, but I've heard that it's totally predictable."

"Oh." I fish in my purse for some gum, but I don't have any. Too bad Natalie's not here. She's always got gum. But I need more than just her gum. If she were here, she'd be cheering me on—and I'd act all embarrassed, but deep down I'd really appreciate it.

"So, you just went to the movie and then went home?" Alex asks.

"What is this? Twenty questions?" Oh, man. Where'd that come from? Just because Natalie and I aren't getting along doesn't mean I need to take it out on Alex. "Alex, I'm sorry. I didn't mean it like that. I'm just, well, nervous about this test and everything. I haven't been practicing much, and . . . what was it you wanted to know?"

Alex sets his jaw. "Nothing. It's just that you weren't at Murphy's. I thought you might show up."

A wiry woman in the drabbest beige suit I've ever seen marches to the front of the room and glances at her clipboard. "Roxy Zimmerman, Charles Mann, your driving instructors are ready for you. Just go out there." She points to a pair of smudged glass doors and then crawls back into her hole.

Alex mouths, "Good luck." I wave at him and follow the Charles guy outside. My cell phone rings to the tune of "Secret Agent Man." Ah, Grandma Perkins.

"I haven't heard from you in a few days, Roxy. How are you doing?"

"Fine! Better than fine, actually. Guess what?"

"What's that?"

"I went out last night. With a guy. And not just any guy, Grandma. A football player." She has a thing for football players. One time, about ten years ago, she even went on a ski vacay with Todd Riggs, back when he was the Broncos' QB. But then Todd signed with the Packers and Grandma wouldn't have anything to do with such a traitor, so she dumped him.

I can't believe I'm dishing to my grandmother like this, but since Natalie isn't exactly fulfilling the role of Roxy's Best Friend, Grandma Perkins will have to suffice.

"That's wonderful, honey. Just remember that you can't fall in love with him. When I first became a Siren, I rarely went on a date with the same man more than once. Twice was tops, until I was positive I could keep my emotions in check."

"Okay." I mean, it's not like I'm going to fall in love with Zach. We're just having some "Summer Lovin'," like Danny says in *Grease*. Oh, God. There I go comparing my life to an eighties movie, just like Natalie. Wait. Wasn't it a *seventies* movie? That's even worse!

I promise Grandma Perkins we'll get together soon and hang up. Two Dodge Neons are parallel parked at the curb. I glance over at Charles, who's so fidgety, he looks like Pumpkin when he needs to be let outside. A man steps out of the front car, a woman out of the back car.

Oh no! I've got to get the male driving instructor or my Siren powers won't work.

I shoot Charles an extra-sweet smile. "FYI, I've heard the woman is a lot easier than the guy. I've been practicing for this test for months, so if you want to go with her, be my guest."

He smiles back. "Really? That's nice of you."

"I know." Whew.

I could say I drove around town—my hands at ten o'clock and two o'clock on the wheel, making smooth stops at stop signs, parallel parking with the prowess of a Beverly Hills limo driver—and legitimately earned an A-plus on my driver's test.

But I'd be lying through my perfectly straight teeth. All I did was sit in the front seat, play my flute, loop a couple of circles around the parking lot for good measure, and the DMV man signed a slip of paper, acknowledging that I passed.

When I walk back into the DMV building, Alex jumps up, his brows knit with concern. "That bad?"

"No, silly. I aced it!" I run over and hug him. Not many guys seem to be the huggy type, but I love hugging Alex. I think it's the way he spreads his hands wide on my back and never lets go until after I do.

I stand underneath the PHOTO sign, feeling all giddy. I'm really getting my license. It's really happening!

"Neeeext," drawls a woman who looks like she forgot to brush her hair this morning. And brush her teeth. I step onto the yellow footprint stickers on the dingy laminate floor and smile for the camera.

A few minutes later a man with a bushy mustache calls my name. He's studying my license like there's something wrong with it. Oh no. Did he somehow find out that I didn't actually take the test?

"What is it?" I ask, holding my palm out.

He doesn't hand it over, though. "In eleven long years of working here, I've never seen anything like it," he mumbles, as if to himself.

"What?" I lean over the counter, but he holds it just out of my reach.

"Janice, come get a load of this," he hollers, and Ms. Bedhead moseys over to have a look. Her jaw drops open and a tinny, high-pitched screech escapes from somewhere inside her boxy body. In no time, a swarm of DMV workers are gawking at my license.

"Excuse me," I say in a loud, demanding tone. "Can I please have my license now?"

Alex sidles up to me and whispers, "What's going on, Rox?"

Mr. Mustache snatches the license from the DMV mob and gives it to me. Finally. "I've never seen such a beautiful driver's license picture," he says, slightly red in the face.

"You should be a model!" Ms. Bedhead gushes.

A *model*?

I can honestly say I've never, *ever* been told I should be a model. I've never even entertained the notion, not in my wildest dreams. Of course, I never dreamed that someday I'd be a Siren, either. But really, why not? I mean, why waste my summer flinging fries at Wendy's when I could be modeling? I mean, I didn't watch all those *America's Next Top Model* episodes for nothing. Besides, it would definitely pay a lot more than fast food, and maybe I'd be able to buy myself a car. I *did* just get my driver's license, after all.

On the way out to Alex's Civic, he tosses me the keys. I try to catch them but miss, and they land on the asphalt with a clank.

"You want me to drive?" I ask, bending down to pick up the keys. "You sure?"

"Sure. You're legal now, right?"

"Right." Well, sort of. I just hope I never have to parallel park. I adjust the seat and stick the key in the ignition. Here goes nothin'.

"Just pull into that gas station over there. I'm running on empty."

"Right."

It takes me a couple of tries to align Alex's car so the gas pump will reach. Okay, so it takes more like five or six, but who's counting? Alex is so sweet; he doesn't even make fun of me. He just hops out and starts filling her up, leaving me a few moments to ponder my future modeling career.

I've heard commercials on the radio about modeling agencies, and I'm sure there are loads of them listed on the Internet. I'll just call a few of the more impressive-sounding ones and make appointments. But first things first. I definitely need to rev up the ol' wardrobe. And who has more fashion sense in her pinky finger than I have in my entire body? Natalie O'Brien, my best friend. Or is she my *ex*-best friend? Are things ever going to be the same between us?

I guess I'll just have to make the first move. Best friends don't throw entire friendships out the window for something as stupid as a party. I pull out my cell and text message her. HEY GIRL. WANNA GO ON A SHOPPING SPREE?

I'm totally psyched about this. Natalie won't be able to turn down shopping, and it'll be a great way to get everything back to normal between us.

Two minutes later my phone beeps and the words GO ASK UR PROUD CROWD FRIENDS appear. My mouth goes dry.

I bite my lower lip and type, I'D RATHER

GO W/ U but I don't send it. Instead, I delete it and send, FINE.

But it's not fine. How could I have been so wrong about Natalie? Besides, there's no way I'm calling up Eva and Amber. I could always call Zach. He's not exactly a fashionista, unless I missed the memo that Nike is the new Versace. But he is my boyfriend. Well, he's almost my boyfriend, right? I mean, we did go on a date. And we did make out. I dial his number. "Hey, Zach."

"Hello? Uh, who is this?"

"It's Roxy." Who does he *think* it is?

"Oh, heeeeey."

"Hey."

"So what's up, beautiful?"

"Not much. Just getting ready to go shopping."

"Ugh. I hate shopping. Well, have fun. I'm off to shoot some hoops with the guys."

"Oh." Okay, so I guess Zach and I aren't hitting the mall. Now what? Isn't he going to ask me out or something? Were we just a one-date wonder? Am I going to have to play my flute every single time I want to do something with him?

"See ya . . ." Oh no! He's going to hang up!

"Er, Zach?"

"Yeah?"

"Want to . . . get a bite to eat a little later?" My heart is beating like crazy. What if he says no?

"Okay, sure. Pick you up at seven?"

"Great."

"Great."

"Okay, bye."

Whew. Close one. For a minute there, I thought maybe he didn't like me.

When I get home, Chase is dusting the blinds in my room. I flop onto my perfectly made bed and watch him for a few minutes. It would be a shame to have to do these tedious chores myself. Especially when Chase does such a great job. I've grown rather fond of having my room and bathroom so sparkly clean and always having freshly washed and pressed clothes to wear. But I did promise my parents I'd talk to him.

I whip out my flute and start playing. Once he's under my spell, I say, "Chase, I want you to continue doing my laundry, keeping my bathroom and room so clean, and doing the dishes . . ." Did I forget anything? Oh, yeah. ". . . and feeding Pumpkin.

But I need you to be very *secretive*. Don't let Mom and Dad notice that you're doing these things. And make sure you're still doing your own chores, and next time someone invites you to a birthday party, go."

Chase's eyes grow big, like when he was seven and I told him the tooth fairy was really a big ugly monster that would gobble him up if his teeth weren't up to its standards. "But . . . what if I'm not done with everything in time?"

I put my hand on his shoulder. "Birthday parties trump doing chores, got it?"

He takes a breath and then smiles. "Got it."

"Good." He turns around and continues his blinds-dusting. "And I really love your new haircut, Chase. Very handsome."

Grandma Perkins whizzes up to the front of the valet line and parks next to the curb. Honking and vulgar hand gestures follow in her wake. It's totally embarrassing, but at least with Grandma around, I didn't have to use my Siren powers on Dad to get him to cough up some spending money. I jump out of her Lexus while she waits for the man in the maroon valet suit to open her door. She looks me up and down and smiles that dazzling smile of hers.

Another man holds the gigantic glass doors open for us as we sashay into Denver's most elite shopping mecca, Designer Palace. In fact, it's so high-end that I've never even stepped foot inside. "I am so pleased you called me, Roxy. I can't remember the last time the two of us went shopping together."

"That's because we never have," I remind her, trying to keep my jaw hinged. This place is amazing! It's like we're traipsing through a royal courtyard, and the stores themselves are part of a beautiful white castle. Above our heads, the ceiling is painted like a sky, complete with wispy clouds and birds.

"Well, that's a shame," she says. "You'd have a much nicer wardrobe if we had." We hop out of the way for a horse-drawn carriage. As it passes, I see two elderly women sandwiched between a mountain of shopping bags.

Despite the hustle and bustle of the shoppers, we get our fair share of rubber-neckers. Will I ever get used to all this attention? Will I ever get used to being a Siren?

Grandma Perkins waves down a guy in a reddish-brown BEAN THERE apron. "Son, would you please bring us one white-chocolate mocha and . . ." She holds her palm out to me, my cue to add my order.

"A French-vanilla iced latte."

He looks at us bleary-eyed and says, "I'm sorry, ladies, but I'm off. The coffee shop's just around the corner, by the big cherub fountain." The guy nods to his left.

Before he can get away, Grandma Perkins starts singing, just loud enough for him to hear. "We'll be in Nordstrom, in the juniors department. You can bring our drinks to us there."

He turns around, gives us a big goofy smile, and literally sprints back to the Bean There shop.

"Ah, that's more like it." Grandma Perkins straightens a button on her tailored linen jacket and winks at me.

"Grandma, we could've gotten the drinks ourselves. It's not a big deal."

For a scary moment she looks like she's going to pinch my cheeks. Instead, she threads her arm through mine and steers me toward Nordstrom. There's a huge mob of people at the other end of the mall. Cameras are flashing, and reggae music is blaring.

"What's going on?" I ask.

"Let's go see."

Come to find out, it's the grand opening of Jaded. Natalie's always lamenting about never getting to go to L.A. or New York, because, up until now, those were the only two American cities deemed cool enough for Jaded. Eva's parents take her to New York to do Christmas shopping, and when she returns with a shopping bag full of Jaded clothes, Natalie's green with envy. She'd pay a hundred bucks for the shopping bag alone.

A twentysomething dressed like Gwen Stefani breezes past us, and when I see the bag she's toting, I get what Natalie's talking about. It's a big iridescent jade-colored circle, kind of like a hatbox, and the handles are silver chains. IS SHE OR ISN'T SHE? is printed on one side in graffiti-style lettering, and JADED on the other.

When Grandma and I get closer, I see that the music isn't coming from a CD as I had assumed. It's live. Am I imagining things, or is that Astra 8 It? Alex *loves* that band! I dig out my cell phone, taking care that my flute doesn't fall out of my purse, and text-message him: ASTRA 8 IT IS AT DESIGNER PALACE. COME NOW!!!

Then I send: JADED IN DENVER! GRAND OPENING AT FASHION PALACE. COME NOW!!! to Natalie.

Before I have a chance to put my phone away, it beeps and there's a message from Alex: I'M AT WORK. CAN'T GET OFF.

SAY U HAVE A STOMACHACHE OR SOMETHING. U CAN'T MISS THIS! I type back.

NO CAN DO he text-messages me. UNDERSTAFFED. THANKS, THO. I'm disappointed, but I knew deep down that Mr. Work Ethic wouldn't ditch his job for this.

Grandma Perkins and I dance to the next song, having such a great time together. I glance at my cell, just in case another text message sneaked through unnoticed. Nope. God, Natalie is being so lame. I can't believe she'd let our tiny little misunderstanding get in the way of something as big as this. I mean, this is *huge*. You know, like the Broncos winning the Super Bowl!

Suddenly, a Hugh Grant look-alike taps me on the shoulder. "Excuse me, miss. I couldn't help noticing that you have a great look. Allow me to introduce myself. I'm Philip Stanford, a talent scout for Envision Modeling Agency of Denver." He holds out a shiny gold business card.

Grandma Perkins snatches the card, studying it for a few seconds. "She does have a great look, doesn't she?" she says, pressing the card into my outstretched palm.

"You must be the proud mother," Philip says, beaming at her.

Grandma chuckles demurely. "You're a charmer, that's for sure. I'm her *grand*mother."

The talent scout clears his throat and then grins at me. "You won the genetic jackpot, young lady." Ha! If he only knew. . . . "Have you ever thought about being a model?" he asks.

I look at Grandma, but she's busy digging for something in her purse, pretending not to be listening. "Not until very recently," I admit.

"That's great news. Well, dear, you simply must call the agency and arrange an interview. The number is on the card"—he taps the business card that I'm holding in the air like a total nerd—"I'm sure we could book you more work than you'd ever believe possible. And what is your name, dear?"

"Roxy Zimmerman."

"Well, Roxy Zimmerman," he says, "I'll let you in on some fabulous news. Envision has been selected to represent Jaded on a local level. Even an international fashion company like Jaded recognizes the quality of our talent, you see. In fact, we're doing a runway show for Jaded right here next weekend," he says, pointing at the floor beneath his shiny wingtips. "There will be live TV coverage by Fox 31 News and the Style Network. Rumor has it, *Seventeen* magazine will be here as well." He pauses to smile at me and I'm gaping. Oops.

"Well, sorry to ramble on," he says, more to Grandma Perkins than to me, "but as you can tell, it's going to be a big to-do and we're all very excited to be a part of it. Now, Roxy," he says, turning his attention back to me. "Give us a call. I look forward to seeing you." And with that, he disappears into the throng.

Grandma finishes dabbing on a bit of lipstick and smacks her lips together. "So, you want to be a model?" she asks, raising one of her delicate eyebrows.

"Might be fun." I smile, imagining my gorgeous Siren face on the cover of *Seventeen*.

"Well, I think that's a fine idea." She leans in to whisper in my ear, "And with your Siren powers, the sky's the limit. New York, L.A., Paris, Milan . . ." Then she stands tall again, winks at me, and says, "Now, let's go into this store and see what all the fuss is about, shall we?"

Ten

Right as we walk through the jade green doors, a man with spiky hair jumps in front of us. "Welcome to Jaded. My name is Sebastian, and I'm the store manager. How can I help you two lovelies?" he says, doing an energetic little bow.

I giggle, still on a high from being "discovered." "We're just looking."

Grandma makes a huffing noise. "We most certainly are not 'just looking.' I'm taking my granddaughter shopping, and we're going to buy her an entire wardrobe. As you can plainly see," she says, gesturing at my faded Roxy tank and shabby jeans, "she's in dire need of an intervention."

"Well, you've come to the right place.

I'll get a dressing room ready for you and we'll get started."

Racks of clothes line the jade-colored walls, and in the center of the store is a posh lounge area, where a group of middle school girls have made themselves comfortable. There are black chairs and couches with metal frames on a multi-colored-striped rug. In the middle of the lounge area sits a sleek glass coffee table displaying neat stacks of fashion mags. The dressing rooms are really cool too. They have frosted glass doors so when someone's trying on clothes, you can see her silhouette.

Grandma watches Sebastian stride toward the dressing rooms and then whispers in my ear, "Pick out anything you want, honey. I'll just sing a little song for that handsome Sebastian fellow and get it *gratis*." She takes my hand in hers. "This is going to be so much fun!"

An hour later Grandma and I exit the store through its jade-colored doors, an over-size shopping bag in each of our hands. My closet will be bursting at the seams with my new Jaded wardrobe. Aha! Eat your heart out, Eva and Amber. There's a new fashionista at Franklin High. "I could definitely get into this shopping thing, Grandma. What a rush!"

She laughs her musical, fluttery laugh as we muscle our way through the crowd that's still gathered around Designer Palace's newest addition. "Sebastian told me they've got numerous styles only available in Paris, so I asked him to have those shipped to your house."

"Really?" I glide past the group of Goth chicks hanging out by the stage where the band was playing earlier. "Wow, that's cool." Natalie would be in seventh heaven. Too bad she's not here. I check my phone one more time, but there's still no response from her.

"All this shopping has made me awfully thirsty," Grandma says. "Oh! I forgot about that boy bringing us our coffee drinks. He was taking them to Nordstrom, wasn't he?"

"The juniors section," I remind her. "But he wouldn't still be there . . ." As the words lift off my tongue, I realize that he's definitely going to be there. After all, he's under Grandma Perkins's Siren spell. Poor guy. "Well, the drinks will be all gross by now. We'll have to get new ones."

Grandma Perkins waves down a carriage, which immediately stops right in front of us.

We clamber in and ride across the mall to Nordstrom. As we're walking in, my cell phone rings. Oh, wow! It's Zach. It's really him! "Hi, Zach," I say, a little too loudly. Grandma Perkins stops prattling on about her new trendy outfits (she saw how cute Jaded clothes looked on me and had to get a few outfits for herself) and raises a perfectly shaped eyebrow.

"You said you wanted to get something to eat. Do you still want to?" Zach asks over the phone.

"Sure!"

"Pick you up at seven."

I hang up and take my not-so-iced latte from the barista who's snoring beside a mannequin display. Grandma Perkins slips a fifty-dollar bill in his pocket without waking him up.

"We have one more item of business while we're here," she says. We pitch our cups in a little trash can behind a cash register, and then she leads me to the accessories department. "You simply must get rid of that atrocious excuse for a handbag." She flashes her dazzling smile at the distinguished-looking man behind the purse counter and he nods.

"May I be of assistance, ladies?"

She swipes my satchel off my shoulder and holds it up between her thumb and first finger like it's a dead skunk. "My granddaughter needs a new handbag, as you can plainly see. Something big enough for this," she says, pulling out my flute.

He blinks a few times and then fumbles with his nautical-themed tie. Once he's convinced that it's acceptably straight, he bends down and selects a purse out of the too-expensive-to-have-out-in-the-open case. It has a really fun, funky print of large starlike flowers in red, brown, turquoise, and cream, with skinny leather straps. "It's an Emilio Pucci tote, made in Italy. We just got this one in two days ago, and I'm certain it'll be all the rage with my young, fashion-forward customers." He hands it to me and then examines his fingernails.

"It's soft. Is it . . . velvet?"

The man shakes his head. "Believe it or not, it's corduroy. Isn't it fabulous? Each tote is distinctly unique. No two are alike. Just like no two women are alike," he says, gesturing to Grandma and me.

When I flip over the price tag, I just about faint. It's almost a thousand dollars!

"If you like it, it's yours," Grandma

Perkins says, winking at me. "Now be a dear and give this to the valet." She hands me the claim ticket. "I'll be there in a jiffy."

What an awesome day! Not only did I get noticed by a talent scout, I'm going out with Zach Parker, the hottest guy ever, *again*. And I can't wait to wear one of my new Jaded outfits!

By the time the valet brings Grandma Perkins's Lexus to the curb, she's handing me my new tote. "Did you just sing for that salesman?" I ask.

"Come to find out, he's gay. Thankfully, the store manager isn't, and it worked like a charm on him."

I duck into her car and say, "Hit it, Grandma. I've got a busy night ahead of me." And then I empty my old purse and put everything in my new Pucci tote. Everything fits, even my flute, fully assembled.

"Where do you want to go?" Zach asks, tucking his sandy hair behind his ear. I'm sitting beside him in his truck in my driveway, buckling up my seat belt. He looks scrumptious in a light blue polo shirt (that matches his eyes) and charcoal gray slacks. I should be psyched about this date, but there's one tiny thing that's totally bugging me.

He honked.

That's right. I was waiting inside like a good little date, full of anticipation and freshly lip-glossed, when I hear this really loud and obnoxious *honk-honk-honk-honk-honk*!" The whole freaking neighborhood heard it.

Chase, who was folding my T-shirts in the privacy of his room, yelled, "Your date's here!"

Mom peered at me over her book. "You're going out tonight?"

"Just going to dinner with Zach."

She put the book down in her lap. Thankfully, she just smiled and said, "That's nice, honey. Be careful. And be home before midnight."

And then Zach honked *again*.

I darted outside and leaped into his muddy truck before the neighbors called the police for a noise infraction or something. I took a deep breath and smiled at him. It's not his fault. It's Eva's. After all, she's the one who put up with this crap before I ever came along. Well, lucky for me, I have my Siren powers. I can whip

Zach into shape with a twitter of my flute.

I don't live in a 1950s bubble or anything. It's just that the honking thing has me in shock. I mean, it wasn't a quick little "I'm here" honk. It was more of a "Get the hell out here" honk. I wouldn't lay on the horn like that if I were picking Zach up for a date. I wouldn't even lay on the horn like that if I were picking Chase and his minions up from a Harry Potter party. Okay, okay. I'll quit obsessing about the honking issue now. Really.

"Did I tell you how beautiful you look tonight?" he asks, taking in my Jaded dress. It's a deep magenta with a plunging neckline, a spiderweb of spaghetti straps, and a row of ripped taffeta on the bottom. It's definitely the poshest thing that's ever touched my skin.

"Thank you." I gaze at him from underneath my long, curly lashes.

He smiles. "You're really gorgeous, you know."

"Stop it," I say, meaning it. He's sounding like my Evanescence CD, the one that keeps repeating the same line over and over again because Pumpkin thought it was a Frisbee and left teeth marks on track five.

Zach just grins. "I can't believe I'm going out with you again."

"Really? Why's that?" Ah, now we're getting somewhere.

"Well, 'cause you're so beautiful." Or not. Argh! Who would've thought that I'd get sick of Zach Parker complimenting me? Can't he think of anything else to say? Like that I'm funny or smart or smell good? That I'm his favorite person to hang out with or talk to? Wouldn't he like to find out if we like the same movies or music or baseball team?

"Did you have fun when we went to the movie?" I ask, digging for a topic that doesn't revolve around my looks.

"I was stoked to be with someone as hot as you, that's for sure."

We're getting absolutely nowhere. Not only are we stuck in a conversational black hole, we're still parked in my freaking driveway.

"Let's go to Murphy's. It's on Littleton Boulevard."

He nods, flips on the stereo, and starts driving. I stare out the window, the cars and trucks blurring like a photo taken with a slow shutter. It's totally stuffy in Zach's truck, and it smells like how I'd imagine the boys' locker room would. I roll down the window and let the wind blast my face. Zach is rambling on about last night's Rockies game, but it's like he's speaking a foreign language.

Why did I chose Murphy's, of all places? Maybe it's because I miss it. Or 'cause I know it serves good, basic, all-American food, and my stomach just doesn't feel up to sushi or escargot or anything fancy.

As soon as Zach pulls into the potholed parking lot, I spot Natalie's yellow Sportage and change my mind.

"Actually, I'm kind of sick of this joint. How about we go to the Olive Garden? They have really good . . . breadsticks."

"What?"

"If you didn't blare your music, you'd be able to carry on a conversation," I say, getting more irritated by the minute.

"Did you say something?"

"Never mind." What's the worst that can happen? Natalie's already mad at me, so it's not like my showing up here is going to change anything. Besides, I'm going to have to face her sooner or later.

Natalie sees us the instant we step into the familiar black-and-white-tiled hangout. She slams her hands on the table of our regular booth and springs up, her brown flippy hair taking on a life of its own. Like Medusa's.

"What are *you* doing here?" she demands. Ginny, Carl, and Fuchsia whip around to see who she's talking to. Hey, where's Alex? Maybe he had to work tonight.

I'm suddenly aware I'm way overdressed for a place like Murphy's. There's gotta be thirty people in here, and everyone's staring. Well, except for the biker chicks at the pool table.

"Just getting a bite to eat. That okay with you?"

"Sure," she says, an impish smile spreading across her berry-tinted lips. "Just don't think you'll be sitting at *our* booth."

Zach makes a "Who are these people?" face and I snap, "Why would we sit with you guys when there's an empty booth over there?" As I grab Zach's wrist and lead him to the table, I force myself not to look back. I don't think I can handle seeing Natalie's face right now.

How long is this stupid feud going to last? I mean, Natalie's biggest dream is to be accepted by the Proud Crowd. And she *knows* I've had a crush on Zach Parker for eons. Why can't she just be happy for me? Why does she always have to make everything about *her*?

"You all right?" Zach asks, grabbing a Murphy's menu from behind the metal napkin dispenser.

"Yeah, why?"

"Don't let those band geeks get to you, Roxy. They're just jealous. You'll get used to it. I hardly even notice it anymore."

I'd like to say that Zach and I are having a marvelous time getting to know each another over the best French fries in town, but, sadly, that's not how it's going down. He's just sitting there, ogling me like I'm some kind of pinup girl, dunking his fries in my ketchup.

"Sweet Home Alabama" rains through the overhead speakers, and my mood instantly improves. I glance over at the jukebox, and there's Alex, wearing his too-short movie uniform pants and the Avalanche T-shirt I gave him for his b-day last fall.

He beelines over to Natalie and the gang and I hear him say, "Hi, guys. What's up?"

With his mouth full of cheeseburger,

Zach mumbles, "Hard to believe you used to be one of them," nodding at their booth.

"What do you mean?" I ask, karate-chopping the ketchup bottle a few times and then giving it a good hard jiggle. If Zach's going to use all my ketchup, the least he can do is squirt some more on my plate.

"You used to be a BeeGee." He studies my face and then adds, "But it's okay, 'cause you're not anymore."

"How do you figure?" I ask. Oops, that's enough ketchup. The waiter is going to have to refill this bottle before the night's over.

"You're with me now. And you're so good-looking—"

"Right." I am with Zach now, and I am pretty. So why aren't I walking on air? I mean, being seen everywhere with Zach and the make-out action is fun and everything . . . just not what I expected. I wish I knew why; I mean, what else could a girl want?

"Sweet Home Alabama" wraps up. Knowing Alex, the next song will be something by Van Halen. Or possibly U2. That old jukebox hasn't been updated since the eighties.

As I take a long drag of my Diet Coke, my gaze floats over to their booth yet again.

Alex's face is pink and jolly as he talks, his hands gesturing wildly. Everyone seems to be really into whatever story he's telling. The instant my eyes lock with Alex's, he doesn't look quite as jolly anymore.

I blink and look over at Natalie, who's sitting next to him. When she sees me, her eyes narrow, and she scoots out of the booth. Looks like she's heading to the ladies' room.

I tell Zach, "Be right back," and dash after her.

She's leaning over the sink, putting on lipstick with short, fierce strokes. A tear rolls down her cheek. In a soft voice, she says, "Why do you always have to rub it in my face?"

"I don't know what you're talking about."

"If you're going to hang out with the Proud Crowd, the least you can do is stay away from our hangout."

"It's not like I'm hanging out with *them*. I'm hanging out with Zach." I try to catch her eye in the smudged mirror, but she looks away. I never knew a soap dispenser could be so riveting. "Under all that brawn and beauty, he's a nice guy. You should get to know him." That's what I keep telling myself, anyhow. But I'm not so sure I believe it.

She snorts. "As if."

"You could've at least responded to my text message this morning," I say, squeezing in beside her to check my hair. Oh, right. Perfect as usual.

"I didn't get it," she says through clamped lips.

I catch her eye in the mirror. "Of course not."

"No, seriously. I didn't get it." She sighs. "My mom won't pay my cell phone bill till I get a job."

She digs a piece of gum out of her Kate Spade knockoff and flicks it into her mouth. Without offering me any.

"Why are you so mad at me?" I ask.

"You want the abridged version?"

I shrug. "I'm all ears."

Natalie holds up a finger. "First of all, you totally sold me out at that party. You acted all embarrassed to be associated with the likes of me. That makes you a two-faced *bitch*, my dear." She gives me a second to process her slam before holding up a second finger. "Two, you're a *liar*. And that's even worse, in my book. It's hard to be friends with a liar."

Oh no! Does she know about the Siren

thing? My pulse races. *Calm down, Roxy.* There's no way she could know. "What are you talking about? I haven't lied to you!"

"Well, if you're not hanging out with the Proud Crowd, why did Eva let you wear her hair clip? And is that Eva's dress, too? She doesn't even loan her new clothes to Amber."

I'm so stunned, I don't know what to say. She really thinks I'm in tight with Eva. Which, if you think about it, is kind of funny. But even if it were true, why's Natalie so pissed about it? She can't tell me that if Eva offered *her* a chance to borrow something from her closet, she'd turn it down.

Natalie pops her gum and reaches out to touch the silky fabric. "Jaded's fall collection, am I right? It's the one on *Lucky*'s 'Must Have' list." She swings the door open and, before stomping out, glowers at me over her shoulder. "Not that *you* would know."

Alone in the bathroom, I whisper at the closed door, "Well, if you were just a tad more civil to me, you could've come over to my house and seen the new fall collection up close and personal." But even though my words are all tough and bitchy, I'm miserable. I miss Natalie in a big way.

I turn to look at my reflection in the mirror—something I do a lot these days. Behind all the beauty, is the old Roxy in there somewhere? The one who deserved to be best friends with Natalie O'Brien?

Eleven

When I go into the kitchen for breakfast the next day, my dad's reading the *Denver Post*, gulping his orange juice.

"Oh, good morning, honey. Would you like some coffee?"

"Sure." I grab a cup out of the cabinet and the bottle of vanilla Coffee-mate out of the fridge. As he fills my cup for me, I suppress the urge to suggest he match his shoes to his pocket protector.

"So, how did your driving test go?" he asks, peering at me over his newspaper.

"Great," I say, stirring my coffee. "It was actually pretty easy. Guess I'm a natural. And it's kinda funny you mentioned it, because I was just going to ask you about a car. You know, something to putt around in now that I'm an official licensed driver and everything."

Since Natalie and I aren't exactly getting along, it's not like I can just call her up and ask her for rides like I'm used to doing. There's always Alex, I suppose. He's such a sweetie; he'd drive me anywhere I'd want to go. But with him working two jobs and all, I doubt he'd be able to moonlight as my on-call chauffeur. Plus, he looked at me all weird at Murphy's, and I can't help wondering if Natalie has recruited him for the Roxy Haters Club. That leaves Zach. And to be perfectly honest, I'm getting really sick of riding in Zach's truck. Has the guy never heard of a car wash?

Dad clears his throat, like he always does right before delivering less-than-wonderful news. Oh no. If I don't get a car of my own, I'm screwed!

I beam at him, giving him my best I'm-such-a-good-daughter look. "It doesn't have to be anything fancy," I say brightly. "Natalie gets along just fine in her little Sportage. And Dad, you have to admit I'm doing great in school. I mean, I got all As last year. Well, except for that B in geometry. Oh, and that

C in my track gym class, but that was only one credit. And it's not my fault I get cramps in my side every time I run more than two laps." I stare down into my coffee cup. It's obvious I'm not getting anywhere with this. I know he's going to tell me I can't have a car until I get a job and earn enough money to buy one myself. That's just the way Dad is: unwaveringly pragmatic, left-brained, and sensible.

Dad clears his throat again, folds the newspaper, and lays it down on the table. Here it comes. Drum roll, please . . .

"Honey, you *do* get good grades, and I *am* very proud of you . . ."

I take a deep breath and try to wipe the disappointment out of my emerald green eyes. But wait! I lean forward and grab his hand. "And not only are my grades good, I've been practicing very hard on my flute. You won't believe how good I've gotten. Hang on, I'll show you!" I jump up, run into my room to get my flute case, and zip back into the kitchen.

Dad's at the sink, rinsing out a coffee mug.

"Do you want to hear this new song I learned?" I ask.

He gives me a half grin and takes a seat. Aha. Like a sitting duck. He'll never know what hit him.

I take out my flute and start playing. When I can see that his eyes are all weird-looking, I go for it. "Dad, I'd like you to let me use your car anytime I want to."

He shoots off his chair. Oh no. He's not going to hurl fruit at me, is he? "Honey, I'm going to give you the keys to my Porsche. I'll just take the bus."

My jaw drops to the kitchen floor. Did he just say . . . ? Am I hearing things? This is off the hook!

I snap my mouth shut and then grin as if Dad's letting me use his car (and volunteering to take the bus, no less) is totally normal. "Thanks, Dad. That's very generous of you."

Mom comes in right when Dad is handing me his keys. She shoots him the evil eye and taps her foot, clearly upset. "Stan, what are you doing?"

"Well, dear, we happen to have an exceptional daughter, and I feel it's time we reward her."

"But your *Porsche*?" Mom says. "May I remind you Roxy just got her license? What if something happens?"

Dad chuckles. "Merrilee, don't be ridiculous. I trust her. She passed her driver's test with flying colors. There's nothing to worry about."

Mom pours herself a cup of coffee, but there's barely any left. She opens the drawer to get a coffee filter and then slams it shut. "Well, I just think we should discuss this."

"I'd love to stay and chat," I say cheerily, "but I've got an interview." I twirl the key ring on my finger, grab my magical flute, and make a beeline for the garage. Getting Dad's car was so easy! A girl can get used to this.

There's a beautiful Paris Hilton–esque girl behind the mahogany desk. A gigantic black sign that reads ENVISION MODELING AGENCY in sleek white letters hangs on the wall behind her, and a song by Dashboard Confessional (or a band that sounds just like them) is droning softly.

"I'm Roxy Zimmerman. I have an appointment." I reach up to smooth my hair and catch a glimpse of my reflection in a big framed mirror on the far wall. Huh. How can my hair look so perfect when I just drove here in Dad's convertible? Don't Siren locks ever get windblown?

The front door opens, and a blaze of sunlight temporarily blinds me. A petite, stocky man in a pin-striped suit breezes past the desk, his shiny wing-tips squeaking on the slate floor. The receptionist straightens her posture and chirps, "Good afternoon, Mr. Valdez."

He comes to a screeching halt and turns around. "And who have we here?"

I glance over my shoulder, but there's no one there. *Me?* "Um, Roxy Zimmerman."

"She has an appointment with Janna." The receptionist fills him in, tapping her bejeweled, manicured finger on the computer screen. "Looks like Philip invited her."

Mr. Valdez strokes his mini-goatee as he looks me up and down. "Tell Janna I'll take this one."

The receptionist's eyes widen and she does as she's told. "Come with me," Mr. Valdez says, leading me down a long hallway wallpapered with thousands of head shots in uniform black frames. Even though the man can't be more than five foot four, I'm having a difficult time keeping up with him in these heels. A gorgeous guy in head-to-toe black steps out of one of the rooms and nods his greeting to Mr. Valdez as he strides toward the reception desk.

I wish I'd worn something a little less . . . flowery. This bright pink sundress with little white roses seemed like a good idea a couple of hours ago. After all, it *is* upbeat and attention-grabbing. But now that I'm here, I'm kicking myself. (Natalie wouldn't have let me leave the house in this thing.) Besides, my new Pucci tote clashes big-time. Ugh.

After following Mr. Valdez into a small square office, I take a seat on the über modern couch. There are several leather portfolios fanned out on the coffee table. One of the walls is made entirely of glass, overlooking a runway in a large empty room.

"That's where our models learn to walk the runway. Our coach, London McGill, previously worked in New York for Ford Models. If we decide to sign you, you'll be required to pass an extensive test before we'll place you on Envision's runway team." He makes himself comfy in his black leather chair and then steeples his fingers on the glossy desktop. Next to his Mac is a nameplate that reads: ANTONIO VALDEZ, AGENCY EXECUTIVE AND FOUNDER.

"Roxanne, was it?"

I look up and show him what I hope is my most dazzling smile. "Roxy."

"Well, I'm glad you're here, Roxy. Philip never disappoints. Now, let's get down to business. Let's see your portfolio."

I fix him with a blank stare.

"You do have a portfolio, don't you?"

"No."

"Do you have a head shot?"

I shake my head.

His forehead crinkles ever so slightly, disproving my assumption that he's a walking Botox ad. "Have you ever done any modeling, Roxy?"

"Uh, nooo." I'm totally unprepared for this. It's like I'm at a band concert when I don't know any of the music *and* I have to do a solo!

He slides open a drawer in his filing cabinet and extracts a lavender piece of paper. "Here's a list of photographers whom we work with. Arrange a photo shoot with one of them and then bring your pictures here so we can see what you've got."

"How long will that take?" I ask, taking the paper from him.

"Most are booked out four to six weeks. But you must have a portfolio of sorts before we can send you out. A nice head shot at the very minimum. I'm sorry, but there are no exceptions. No matter how beautiful you are."

Four to six weeks? He's gotta be kidding me! The summer will practically be over by then. And if the Jaded fashion show is this weekend, I've got to get cranking. I don't even have a recent photo of myself, let alone a professional head shot. But wait . . .

"Actually, I *do* have a head shot." I reach into my tote and grab my flute. I start playing, filling the room with beautiful music. I'm a Siren, and I'm not going to let a little thing like a head shot keep me from starting my modeling career. When Mr. Valdez is unmistakably under my spell, I put the flute away and hand him my driver's license. "Here it is. Amazing, isn't it?"

Driving home from my interview, I spot Alex sitting on the stairs in front of his tan stucco house, yo-yoing. He's wearing a pair of long shorts and an Auto Spa T-shirt, a bag of Skittles in his hand.

I pull over to the curb and break.

He stands up and jogs over. "I never thought I'd see the day *you* were driving this. What, did your dad get a new one or something?"

"Nah. He just lets me buzz around in it 'cause I get good grades and all." I know I said I'd stop lying but it's not like I can say, "I'm a Siren and I used my powers on my own father."

"Wow." He whistles, running his finger over the hood. "You know, I get pretty decent grades too. Are your parents interested in adopting a trombone player with a 3.8 GPA?" He holds up his bag of candy. "Want some?"

I nod, and he pours some Skittles into my palm. I pop a green one and a purple one into my mouth.

"Maybe if I were your adopted brother, I'd get to see you more often," he says. "You know, for meals and pillow fights and whatnot."

"I'll be sure to ask them if they're in the market for another mouth to feed."

Alex pours the remaining candies into his mouth, then balls up the empty Skittles bag, tosses it high in the air, and catches it behind his back.

"Impressive."

He grins, his smile slightly lopsided.

"Thanks. One of my better talents."

"So, what're you up to today?" I ask, sliding my sunglasses on top of my head.

He shoves his hands in his front pockets and rocks back and forth on his heels, nodding at the lawn. "Just giving this baby a good mowin' job."

"I'm sure if I mention to Dad that you mow lawns, he'll adopt you in a flash."

"Yeah, well, if I hadn't waited till we needed a machete just to get to the front door, it wouldn't have been a big deal. But when I saw the UPS guy's mug on the carton of milk this morning, I knew I had to dust off the ol' mower, push up my sleeves, and get dirty."

"I'm sure the UPS guy will be mighty grateful when his knight on shiny mower comes to rescue him."

Alex smiles. "So, enough about me. What's up with you?"

"Nothing nearly as exciting as cutting grass. But I'm just getting back from an interview. I'm going to be a model," I say, a tad more enthusiastically than I'd intended.

"Cool! Just think—I get to say 'I knew her when' when you're gracing the pages of the Victoria's Secret catalog in a pair of

sweats with PINK written all over the butt."
I stare at him until his cheeks turn red and
he says, "Yeah, I've been known to flip
through a catalog or two. It's kinda hard not
to when my mom and sisters get them in
the mail every Monday, Wednesday,
Thursday, and Saturday." He scratches his
shoulder. "Not that I keep track."

"I don't think you'll see me in the
Victoria's Secret catalog any time soon. But
I do get to be in a fashion show at Designer
Palace on Saturday."

"Really? Saturday, eh? Well, I'd love to
come cheer you on——"

For a brief moment I visualize Alex
McCoy standing beside the runway, holding
up one of those big Styrofoam hands that
reads ROXY'S #1! and trying to get the
whole mall to partake in the wave.

"——but I'll be at the PAD. Benjamin
says hi, by the way. And so do Rosie and
Eleanor. They wanted to know where you
were last weekend."

"Oh, yeah? Um, well, I kinda spaced it.
Sorry. Probably all the excitement of it
being . . . the day after my birthday."
Smooth, Roxy, real smooth.

He looks at me kind of funny for an

instant and then shrugs. "It's not the same without you. Rosie and Eleanor were fighting over who got to walk the big white poodle again, and I don't do nearly as good a job refereeing as you do."

"Well, I'll have to check my schedule. Now that I've started modeling, I'll probably be pretty busy on Saturdays." Truth is, even though I'm excited to get my modeling career going, I'm going to miss volunteering. I'm going to miss the old people, the poor orphan dogs, and . . . hanging out with Alex. "You know what?" I say. "I'm totally craving a Slurpee. Wanna come with? My treat."

"Sure!" Alex hops into the passenger seat and fastens his seat belt. We cruise through the neighborhood in silence. A little boy's basketball escapes and bounces into the middle of the road. I stop and he runs after it.

After the boy is safely back to his driveway, I say, "Hey, Alex?"

"Yeah?"

"So . . . I haven't seen Natalie in a while. How's she doing?" I ask as nonchalantly as possible.

He shrugs. "Same ol'."

"My grandma got me all these cool clothes from Paris and they just arrived yesterday. I want to give a bunch to her because I know she'll love them, especially to wear when school starts and everything."

"Yeah, she'd really like that," Alex agrees.

"But, well, if you haven't noticed, we're not exactly talking these days," I say as I turn onto Mountain Boulevard.

Alex shrugs. "Yeah, I noticed. Actually, everyone noticed. You two used to be inseparable."

I decelerate and then stop as a yellow light turns red. "Do you think you could take them to her? The clothes, I mean. I could give them to you and you could . . ."

He just shakes his head.

"I've already tried to apologize, Alex." The light turns green and I slip the stick shift into first. But I pop the clutch and the car lurches forward, sputters, and dies. Someone in a black Escalade lays on the horn, and I feel the sweat beading on my forehead. Finally, I get the Porsche restarted and hit the gas.

"You should try again," Alex says as the Escalade driver whizzes around us, giving me the finger. "Don't give up."

I sigh. "Well, here we are. Seven-Eleven."

We're over at the Slurpee machine and I'm teaching Alex how to make the perfect Slurpee (the poor boy didn't realize you're supposed to put the lid on before filling up), when Eva and Amber walk in, both sporting tennis skirts. Wonderful.

"Hey, look, it's Roxy!" Amber says to Eva.

"So it is," Eva says, heading straight for us. "Hiya, Roxy. What're you up to?"

Hmm. Very interesting. So Eva's decided to be nice to me now? That's cool, I guess. A girl can never have too many friends, right?

"What she really wants to ask is, 'Are you and Zach still together?'" Amber says, practically jogging to catch up with her long-legged friend.

Eva rolls her eyes and flips her long blond hair behind her shoulder. "What*ever* I'm so over Zach it's not even funny. Now be a sweetie and get me a sugar-free Red Bull." She pushes Amber in the direction of the energy drink section and then turns her dark blue eyes on me.

"So, *are* you still dating what's-his-face? We haven't seen you with him lately. Oh, or are you with *this* guy now?" She lifts her chin to indicate Alex, who has red Slurpee dribbling down his arm and splattering all over the floor.

When Alex realizes that Eva and I are staring at him, he chuckles nervously. "I, um, thought I was supposed to overfill it 'cause of the shrinkage factor. Isn't that what you said to do, Rox?"

I clear my throat and take a few steps away from the sticky puddle. "Alex is just a friend."

Eva nods and then snatches the silver can that Amber just brought her. "I said *sugar-free*," Eva snaps, passing the can right back to Amber. Amber skedaddles to make the exchange. Eva eyeballs my Slurpee. "How do you drink those things and say so thin?"

Before I can think of an answer, she says, "Well, it's been nice chatting with you. But we've gotta run now. We've got a court reserved at the club."

I watch the two girls pay for their drinks and parade out to Eva's baby blue Mustang while a twentysomething guy in a striped shirt mops up Alex's mess.

Alex holds a Slurpee cup up for me to

inspect. "Look, I think I have the hang of it," he says, smiling.

"Good job," I say, and I pay the cashier.

Back in my dad's Boxster, Alex is staring down at his Slurpee, wiggling the straw up and down and making an obnoxious squeaky sound. "Something bothering you?" I ask, slipping on my sunglasses. "I mean, besides the fact that I have a cooler car than you?" I hit him on his arm playfully.

"Do I embarrass you?" he asks.

"What do you mean?"

"You know what I mean."

I take a long swig of my drink, buying time. And getting a major brain freeze in the process. "Alex, there's no use crying over spilled Slurpee. Unless," I add as an after-thought, "it's the last bit of cherry left in the whole machine."

"I'm being serious, Rox."

"What do you want me to say?" I put the Boxster in reverse and back out of the parking spot.

"Just be honest."

I take another sip, even though I'm still suffering from a brain freeze. Does he really want me to say he's sometimes a bit of an embarrassment? I can't tell him that!

Alex plunks his drink in the cup holder and crosses his arms over his chest. "Okay, so here's the deal," he says. "*I'm* going to be completely honest with *you*. If you can handle it, that is."

"Bring it." I shift into third gear, relieved not to be on the spot any longer.

"You and Zach Parker might look good together, but you're not good together."

"What's *that* supposed to mean?"

"You're not right for each other. You're totally different people."

I snort. "Like he's a popular jock and I'm a nerdy band girl?"

Alex slaps the dash. "God, Roxy. Not even. What I mean is, Zach Parker doesn't deserve you. I think you're great. You're *real*." He scratches his nose and then rests his elbow on the top of the door. "At least, you *used* to be real."

I bite my inner cheek, willing myself not to snap. I can't believe Alex McCoy, Mr. Nice Guy, just said something so mean! Thank God for my sunglasses, 'cause I can feel tears welling up in my eyes. "I'm still real," I say, my voice cracking.

"Oh? Then tell me this. Will things be

the same at school? Will we still hang out? Or are you going to ignore me, now that you're in with the V.I.Peeps?"

As soon as the words "Of course we'll still hang out," and "Everything's going to be the same" come rushing out of my mouth, I realize I'm full of crap. And I hate myself for it. I can't stand lying to Alex. "Listen," I say, scrounging up the guts to lay it on the line. "To be honest, I think you might be right. About me and Zach, I mean. It's not really . . . what I expected. I mean, I still think he's cute. But now that I know him better . . ."

I look over at Alex and catch a glimmer of a smile. "Oh, don't look so smug, you jerk!"

"So are you going to break up with him?" he asks as I pull into his driveway.

"I don't know, Alex. What would you do if you were me?"

"Dump him and go out with me."

Is he serious? Nah, he can't be. But what if . . . ?

Twelve

While I'm stopped at the traffic light in front of Designer Palace on Saturday afternoon, I make a decision. I'm going to make up with Natalie, no matter what it takes.

The driver in front of me lays on his horn, apparently upset that the twenty cars in front of him chose not to run that red light.

It's a beautiful summer day: blue sky, clear view of Mount Evans to the southwest, and a perfect roll-the-windows-down eighty-two degrees (according to the digital readout on the rearview mirror). I listen to the *jut-jut-whoosh* of the sprinklers in the park across the street for a minute or two, and then dig my cell out of my tote.

"Natalie," I say into the voice-activated speed dial. It rings four times before she answers.

"I've been meaning to call you," she says by way of greeting.

"Really?" I unwrap my Pop-Tart (strawberry with frosting) and take a bite. Mom keeps these around for Chase, but I have a secret love of them.

"I wanted to thank you for all these great clothes. They're fab."

"Oh, it's no biggie," I mumble with my mouth full. I dropped them off last Wednesday, after going to 7-Eleven with Alex. She wasn't home, so I just let myself into the O'Brien's house (they keep a spare key on top of the back doorjamb) and left them on her bed.

"Why'd you give them to *me?*"

"I knew you'd like them. They're totally *you*. Plus, I was kinda hoping they could be like a peace offering," I admit.

When the car in front of me lurches forward, I stuff the rest of the Pop-Tart in my mouth and hit the gas. An awkward pause reigns over the phone while I chew. How did I ever let things get so bad between us? "Natalie, I'm sorry. I'm sorry I've been such a jerk."

"Me too."

Is she saying she's sorry too—or is she agreeing that I've been a total jerk? Oh, well. It doesn't really matter. "I'm glad we're talking again." If my ego hadn't gotten in the way, I would've apologized for staying at the Proud Crowd party when they'd kicked her and Alex out. I would've apologized for pretending not to be friends with her. All I needed to do was tell her the truth—that I felt slimy about the way I'd treated her—and this stupid war never would've been waged.

"Me too, Rox. It just hasn't been the same without you. I mean, I know you're, like, totally in love and everything, but—"

"Yeah, about that," I say. "I kinda wanted you to think Zach and I were in love. But in reality, he doesn't have much to say on any subject besides sports." *Or how beautiful I look,* I think, but don't say out loud.

"Why'd you want me to think you liked him so much, if he's nothing but a big ol' yawn?" Natalie asks.

Good question.

"I guess I didn't want to admit that I was wrong . . . ," I say softly. And that I'd stayed back at that Proud Crowd party to be with Zach, who, after all, wasn't really worth getting in a big fight with my BFF. "But anyway, I wanted to tell you I decided to try my hand at modeling. Today's my first day. I'm doing a runway show for Jaded. You should come."

"Omigod! *Really?*" I hold the phone away from my ear till she calms down. "I wish I could, but I can't. I don't get off till eleven." She sighs heartily. "I can't stand working at Safeway. All I do is bag groceries, gather carts in the parking lot, and, if I'm lucky, mop up spilled pickles."

I grin, visualizing my friend in an ultra-unfashionable navy blue pinafore. "I didn't even know you had a job, Natalie. How long have you been working there?"

"Today's my second day."

"Well, I hope someone knocks over a jar of pickles just for you."

She laughs. "Gee, thanks."

When I pull into the parking lot, Natalie and I zip through our good-byes and hang up. I know it sounds cliché, but now that Natalie and I are friends again, I feel like a huge weight has been lifted off my chest.

London McGill, Envision's runway coach, claps her hands together three times, and the models look up, giving her their full attention. In a hushed voice, she says, "Ladies, it's time. Please line up like we practiced last night."

Since we're in the mall, there's not a "backstage" for us to hang out in until showtime. So we're stashed behind a big gray screen with JADED painted in graffiti-style, jade-colored letters. Someone turns on the hip-hop music, and as it booms throughout the mall, I dodge a cloud of hair spray and give myself a quick once-over in one of the full-length mirrors. My makeup and hair look amazing, and in slinky silver pants and a tight winter-white cashmere sweater, I look every inch a supermodel. But I don't feel like one.

Even though I've been practicing my runway walk, I still don't have it down. If I hadn't played my flute for Mr. Valdez, London wouldn't have placed me on

Envision's runway team. The other girls aren't exactly Gisele Bündchen clones, but they definitely walk circles around me.

As I take my place at the end of the line, the stylist wraps a deep red loopy knit scarf around my neck. "Are you okay?" she whispers.

I flash her a smile I hope exudes confidence. "Better than ever," I say. *Please don't puke,* I beg my stomach. *Just a few minutes and it'll all be over.*

"Three, two, one," London calls, signaling the start of the show. The first girl disappears around the screen, followed a moment later by the second girl.

The line of models is melting fast and I'm so not ready to do this. Oh no! I'm on! I graze one of the other girls as I step onto the runway, and she shoots me the evil eye. But there's no time to apologize because I'm on. Where did all these people come from? Don't they have jobs and families and other things to do? Can they see my knees shaking?

I take a deep breath and take off, not really sure what my feet are doing way down there. All I know is these heels are impossible to walk in, and it's taking every bit of effort to stay on top of them. Oh, God. I'm going to break my ankles—I just know it!

I concentrate on what London told me when I started working with her just three days ago. Shoulders back, neck elongated, back straight, stomach in, hips rolled forward, arms dangling, legs crossing with every step, facial expression to match the theme of the show. I guess the theme of this show is edgy. Or is it casual? Or is it Colorado's answer to haute couture? I really don't know. Too bad it's not "freaking out." Or "kill your little brother."

Chase is in the audience, jumping up and down and making faces at me. Oh, great. I hope no one knows we're related. Mom is standing beside him, trying to get him to settle down. She flashes me an encouraging smile and gives me a thumbs-up. Note to self: Never share fashion show schedule with family.

Okay, I'm almost done. The end is in sight. Just a little further. . . .

Oh, wait. Isn't that Amber Millan's head poking out from all those shopping bags? Eva must be around here somewhere. Ah, there she is! They're pointing at me and smiling. I hold my head up even higher when I walk past them, trying not to lose my rhythm, trying not to lose the modicum of poise I'm desperately hanging on to. Right before I'm back behind the screen, my heel gets stuck on the hem of my pants. Oh, crap! *Tripping!* I let out a shrill scream, landing awkwardly on the side of my left shoe. Thank God, I catch myself before I fall flat on my heavily made-up face. But my heel snaps and I have to limp the last few feet. Just kill me now.

A moment later Mr. Valdez (Mr. Envision Modeling Agency of Denver himself) appears behind the screen, strutting around in burnished dark jeans and a soft green V-neck. "That was fabulous, everybody. Our best show yet." The girls stop changing back into street clothes long enough to say thanks. He pauses in front of me. "Roxy, we have a photo shoot opportunity that you'll be perfect for. Here's the information." He hands me a slip of paper with HOT-AIR BALLOONING IN VAIL typed across the top and the address, date, and time scribbled underneath.

"Okay," I say, still a bit out of it. "Thanks."

"No problem," he says. "And don't worry about today. Some of our models are a mess on the runway, but really shine through in print ads."

He disappears before I have a chance to ask him to elaborate. Did he mean that I totally sucked today? Or was he just saying that doing print ads might be a more natural fit for someone like me? Nonplussed, I slide off the pointy-toed stilettos before they cause permanent damage to my feet (how some women wear high heels every day I'll never know), slip on my Skechers, and hobble out into the open.

Mom sprints over to me with Chase loafing behind her. "Oh, honey, you did such a great job! I'm so proud of you!" she exclaims, going in for a hug.

Chase mutters, "Mom forced me to come and made me promise to say something nice when you were done. So here goes." He clears his throat. "I'm glad you didn't fall off the runway when you tripped."

And that's precisely when Eva and Amber choose to wander over. "Hi, Roxy," Eva says sweetly. "I didn't know you were a model."

"Well, she just started," Mom pipes in. "She did pretty well for her first time, don't you think?"

"I'm sure with a little more practice, she won't look like she's all constipated," my mutant brother says.

"Oh, and I suppose you go to so many fashion shows, you're an expert?" I say, wishing I could just disappear.

"Do you girls go to school with Roxy?" Mom asks, and I'm so grateful she changes the subject before it gets any more mortifying.

Eva and Amber nod politely.

"That's nice. And what instruments do you two play?"

Oh. My. God.

"Pardon me," a man says. "Would you mind moving over just a little?" Mom, Chase, Eva, Amber, and I shift our little Roxy Embarrassment Session over so a small group of people can carry the gray JADED screen away from the storefront. I recognize the man as Sebastian, the manager of Jaded. An idea pops into my head.

"I'm sorry, but I've got to bail," I say. "Um, it's business."

Mom gives me a confused look and then says, "Okay, but don't be home late. Your father and I would like to spend a little time with you before we leave for our trip."

I dart into the store, dodging fashion-
istas, racks of clothes, and shiny metal man-
nequins as I chase Sebastian through the
store. "Hey, Sebastian!" I holler, and he
whips around. After a beat, a smile spreads
across his clean-shaven face.

"Well, hello there. If it isn't one of my
best customers! So nice to see you." He
glances behind me. "And where is that
lovely grandmother of yours?"

"Out and about, as always. Hey, do you
have a minute? I wanted to ask you something."

"Sure."

Taking Sebastian's arm, I lead him into
the back hall. We head to the employee
break room, where a girl about my age is
checking her hair in a compact mirror.
When she realizes she's not alone, she clicks
her mirror shut and tosses her diet-bar
wrapper into the trash-can. "I'm on my way
out," she informs her boss as she marches
past us, eyeing me a bit suspiciously.

Sebastian and I venture into the empty
break room. I say, "This will only take a
minute." Or less. After all, Grandma
already primed him. I take out my flute.

He squints an eye, apparently thinking

I'm crazy, but nods. I play for about fifteen seconds, until his eyes widen and gloss over. "My friend Natalie O'Brien would love to work here. Please arrange that for her." I tuck my flute back into my purse and then jot down her name and number on the back of a sales slip that someone had left on the table.

"A marvelous idea! Natalie O'Brien will be perfect," he says, gazing at the sales slip as if it's a winning Colorado Lottery ticket.

"Oh," I add as an afterthought, "and make sure she gets a seventy-five percent merchandise discount." Ah, pure genius.

By the time I'm finished with my chitchat with Sebastian, it's pretty dark outside. I fold myself into the Boxster and say "Natalie" into my cell phone's voice-activated speed dial. I've been dying to tell her the good news.

"Hey girl, guess what?"

"Eva's pregnant and she and Zach are having a shotgun wedding? Only the baby isn't really Zach's—it's an alien's."

"Ha-ha. No, seriously. You can quit your job at the grocery store. I've got something you'll like a lot better."

"Oooooooh?"

"Yeah," I say. "The *National Enquirer* is hiring reporters."

"Ha-ha."

"Actually, you've got a job at Jaded."

"Shut up! Are you serious? I've been calling every day to see if someone happened to quit, but they've got, like, a million applications." She pauses and then asks, "How?"

"I just talked to the store manager. I told him how perfect you'd be and he agreed."

"Oh my God, Roxy. This is too cool! You're the greatest! You're the best! You're awesome!"

"I know, I know."

"And did I forget to mention that you're modest?"

I laugh. We chat the whole drive home, even though she's at work. ("Not like it matters if they fire me. I've got a job at Jaded!") It feels so good to catch up with her. She's so psyched to work at her favorite store. It's like she just got crowned Prom Princess.

Thirteen

"Okay, so that's twenty-one forty Harrison Avenue? Great. Thanks, Mrs. Parker."

I close my cell phone and stare at it until a black VW bug honks at me. "I'm going, I'm going," I mutter, stepping on the gas and shoving the phone into my purse.

When I called Zach, his mom told me he was at Eva's house. All the gang is there, she said. She acted a little surprised that I wasn't there already, and even more surprised when I told her I had no clue where Eva lived. Imagine how surprised she'd be if I told her that her son's under my Siren spell, and that's why we've been hanging out. What would she have to say about that?

I pull up to the address Mrs. Parker gave me, and, sure enough, his muddy pickup's parked on the steep circular driveway, along with Eva's Mustang. I yank the parking break so the Boxster won't roll down the hill, then grab my purse and hop out.

The house is a white colonial-style with a gigantic weeping willow in the middle of the yard and a rainbow of geraniums lining the brick walkway. I clank the brass knocker on the dark green door until it opens, revealing Eva in her FHS short shorts and a bikini top.

"Oh hey, Roxy. What're you doing here?" she asks, fiddling with her necklace—a silver chain with a heart locket. Did Zach give it to her back when they were an item?

"I'm here to see Zach." I step inside before she has the chance to invite me in. You know, just in case she *doesn't* invite me in.

Eva peers over my shoulder. "Nice car. It's not yours, is it?"

I shrug. "It's my dad's, but he lets me take it whenever I want, so it's pretty much mine."

"Wow, that's cool."

The Nelsons' house is all velvet and mahogany and wallpaper, smelling of Old

English and old money. According to Natalie, Eva's great-grandparents started the Snowflake Ski shops. And once Eva turns eighteen, she's going to be Denver's newest millionaire. Rough.

Eva leads me down the hall, her bare feet slapping on the rose-colored tile. "Zach's out back. Want anything to drink? A wine cooler, perhaps?"

A lump the size of Jupiter forms in my throat. "Uh, I've been meaning to apologize for, um . . . spilling my wine cooler on your dress. I hope it didn't stain." Did I really think slinging my drink all over Eva would make me feel victorious? What had gotten into me that night at J.T.'s party?

Eva waves her hand dismissively. "Bygones." Then the weirdest thing happens. She actually smiles at me. "I'm really glad you stopped by, Roxy. Before we go outside, can I ask you something?" She takes my hand and leads me to a burgundy love seat in the living room. There's an enormous oil painting of her family on the wall: The distinguished Mr. Nelson, his lovely and well-preserved surgeon wife, and a twelve-year-old Eva Nelson in a dark green sheath and pearls.

"Uh, sure, I guess. . . ." I perch next to her.

"How does it feel?" She's looking at me intensely, like she's waiting for me to reveal the secret of life.

"How does *what* feel?" Is she asking about Zach? Oh, God, I'll die if she asks if Zach and I have had sex.

"To be a model." Eva leans forward, flinging her long blond ponytail behind her shoulder.

My face heats up. "Oh." I set my tote down at my feet. "It's fun, I guess—"

"You were so great at that Jaded fashion show. I was just standing there watching it and I was all, 'I know that girl!'" A huge smile emerges on her face and she clamps her hand on top of mine. "So tell me *every*thing! Don't you dare leave out a single, teensy-tiny detail."

This is all so weird. I mean, Eva's hanging on to my every word. I don't think we've ever even made eye contact before, let alone had a tête-à-tête.

Eva smacks her lips, a dreamy look in her blue eyes. When I wrap up the story of How Roxy Became a Model (leaving out the Siren bits, naturally), she says, "Awesome."

I nod.

"Well," she says, standing up, "I'm sure you're eager to see Zach. I just wanted to live vicariously for a minute."

Huh? Did Eva the Diva just admit to being intrigued by *my* life? And what's more, did she just use a five-syllable word? I'm still pondering these oddities when we go out the sliding-glass doors and find Zach, J.T., Devin, and Amber hanging out around an oval-shaped swimming pool. The yard is full of trees, bushes, flowers—oh, wow, and a barbeque setup that would bring a grown man to tears.

Devin does a majorly splashy cannonball and drenches Amber, who's sprawled out on a lounge chair, sipping lemonade. She screams, but by the look in her eyes, she doesn't seem that upset. By the size of her bikini top, she doesn't seem that modest, either. (If anyone ever wants me to model a bathing suit like *that*, I'm so saying no. Even though my boobs are pretty damn amazing, if I do say so myself.)

J.T. spots me first. "Yo, Zachster. Look who's here."

Zach swims to the ladder and climbs out of the pool, water dripping down his tan, muscular body. He looks like a hunk right out of those cheesy calendars, except he's wearing knee-length board shorts instead of a banana hammock (which are totally disgusting, if you ask me).

Eva tosses Zach a pineapple-patterned beach towel and he dries his eyes and hair. "Hiya, Roxy. What's up?" He gives me a sexy smile and I can't help but wonder if he's going to be smiling after I do what I have to do.

Everybody's watching and listening to us. "Uh, I just wanted to talk. Can we go inside or something?"

He shakes his head like a wet dog. "Sure."

I take him to the love seat where Eva and I were sitting earlier. "Uh, Zach? Maybe you should sit on the towel. You know, so you don't ruin the upholstery? I think it might be an antique." Not that I'd know, but it sure doesn't look like something you can just pick up at American Furniture Warehouse. And I want him sitting down because I'm not sure how he's going to react to what I have to tell him.

"So, what's up?" he asks again, spreading the towel between his wet trunks and the love seat.

"Do you ever get the urge to hang out with

me?" I ask, staring at the fancy chandelier-like light above our heads.

"Sure." He puts his hand on top of mine.

"But everything that happens between us is 'cause I arrange it or ask for it or suggest it." He looks at me as if I'm speaking Chinese. "I suggest we get something to eat, and we do. I ask you to kiss me, and you do."

He kisses me, and suddenly I feel nauseous. The kiss itself is fine. It's the exact same kind he's been giving me since the day I used my Siren powers on him and told him to kiss me like Enrique Iglesias. Is it all he's capable of? Like he's a robot and can only do what I've programmed him to do? Can't he be spontaneous? You know, mix it up a little?

"Do you love me?" I bite my lip, wishing I hadn't just asked him that. Talk about awkward. And not that I'm experienced with this, but I'd guess it's not the best question to ask a guy right before you break up with him.

"Of course I love you, Roxy." He smiles lazily and runs his fingers through my hair.

"Why?"

"Why what?"

"Why do you love me?"

He's still smiling and stroking my hair,

but he looks kinda funny. Like he's reading a Post-it that's stuck to my forehead. "Because you're the most beautiful girl in the whole world."

Okay, fine. I'm not surprised he said that. But I guess I was hoping he would say something else, you know, besides me being pretty.

He's awfully cute, and he's so athletic and popular. What girl wouldn't want to be with Zach Parker?

This girl.

But I *am* fond of the guy. I've been crushing on him forever, and I do want what's best for him. This breaking up thing is totally hard. How can I let him down easy? How can I release him from his Date the Siren duties in a way that leaves his dignity intact? Maybe I can fix him up with someone else—someone who'll make him happy.

I glance up at the painting of the Nelsons and a crazy idea bounces into my skull. What if Zach fell in love with Eva? I mean, they make such a terrific couple. The whole plan is so poetic!

I dig out my flute and start playing, Zach's eyes softening into light blue satin.

"Zach, I want you to get back together with Eva."

Wait a sec.

Will the whole act get old for Eva, like it has for me? I don't want her to be stuck with a Robot Dream Guy for the rest of her life. I don't want my gift of Zach Parker to become a nuisance or a curse.

Eva needs an out. You know, just in case she's not deliriously happy about a total hottie devoting himself to her. It's the least I can do. "If Eva ever tells you she wants to break it off, be a good sport and follow her wishes."

"Roxy?"

"Mmm?"

"I've gotta go. I've gotta talk to Eva."

"Wait a sec. One more thing. Take your truck to the Auto Spa first thing in the morning for the full-service car wash, and take it back at least twice every week. Okay, that should be it for now. See ya later." Ha! I just played matchmaker for the Proud Crowd King and Queen. Never in a million years would I have expected myself to do something like this. As I'm putting my flute away, I see something glittery in the bottom of my purse. Eva's rhinestone hair clip. I place it on the coffee table, right next to the exotic silk flower arrangement.

After Zach flees out of the house, I snatch the beach towel he left behind and hop up on my feet. Through the sliding-glass doors, I see him march right up to Eva and take her in his arms. It's a total Hollywood moment. A tear slides down my cheek, and I use the towel to wipe it away.

As bizarre as it sounds, I think I'm crying from happiness. Zach and I were never meant to be, and I feel so much lighter now that he and Eva are back together. After folding the towel, I slide the door open just a little and set it outside. Before I close the door again, I hear J.T. say, "Dude, so if you aren't with Roxy anymore, is it cool if I go for her?" and I laugh out loud. Then I gather my things and head for the front door.

Eva comes running after me. "Hey, Roxy! You're not leaving, are you?"

"Yeah, I think I'm going to go check on my friend. She just got a new job at Jaded that she's superexcited about."

"Shut up! You know someone who works at Jaded?"

I nod. "Natalie O'Brien."

"That band geek girl you used to hang with?" Eva's dark blue eyes squint disbelievingly.

"Actually, we're hanging out again. And she *is* in band, but she's actually really cool. They'd never hire Natalie to work at Jaded if she were a geek. She's always one step ahead of the latest fashion craze. It's pretty amazing, actually."

Eva is quiet for a beat or two. "Maybe she can help me find a first-day-of-school outfit," she says softly.

I smile. "I'm sure she'd be happy to."

"So what's up with you and Zach?" she asks, refilling the pitcher with lemonade.

I take a few steps backward and lean against the breakfast bar, hoping to look casual. "We're not together anymore."

Eva crinkles her little nose like a rabbit. Finally, she snorts. "He said you broke up with him!"

"Oh, this is *rich*," Amber says as she sidles up to Eva. "I don't think *anyone's* ever broken up with Zach Parker."

"*I* broke up with him," Eva says indignantly. "Remember when he had the nerve to pick me up for prom in his nasty pickup?"

Amber says, "That doesn't count, Eva."

Then she whispers, "You guys *did it* that very night."

"I didn't break up with him," I pipe up. "He told me he has a thing for another girl, so he dumped me. He was totally cool about it, though, no hard feelings or anything."

Eva whispers, "He wants to get back together with me."

I pretend to be pleasantly surprised. "Oh! That explains a lot, then. Well, congrats, Eva."

"You're not pissed?"

"Not at all. You make a great couple. I'm sure you two will be very happy together."

"Are you for real?" Eva asks.

"I hope so," I say to myself as she runs back to her man.

Fourteen

"No parties, young lady." Mom stops digging in her closet and looks at me, making eye contact. "I left a message with Mother, letting her know you're going to be home alone. . . ."

Their huge black suitcase is open on their bed, a bunch of touristy clothes spilling over. "Need any help getting this baby shut?" I ask, thinking it a bit odd that Mom is having Grandma Perkins check in on me instead of Patricia, Alex's mom.

"It's under control, I think," Mom says, parading around in the teddy-bear nightshirt she got at Yellowstone last year. "We've got a system."

"You're not still putting that pair of

rainbow-striped suspenders around it, are you?"

Dad tosses another pair of black socks in the pile and then shakes his head. "The security folks gave us a hard time last time, so I'm afraid we'll just have to make do without the suspenders."

Mom ties a big pink bow on the suitcase handle and steps back to inspect her work. "That'll do. Don't want someone else to take our suitcase by mistake." I pity the people who get their suitcase mixed up with my parents'. They'd have to wear Dad's baggy shorts and black socks and Mom's painfully white tennis shoes.

My parents are spending their twentieth wedding anniversary at Disneyland, where they had their honeymoon. Personally, I think it's kind of weird for them to go to Disney and leave their kids at home. But I'm actually pretty psyched to be left behind. It'll give me time to hang out with friends. Plus, I have that photo shoot coming up on Tuesday.

After passing my Dad the SPF 50 sunscreen, I retire to my bedroom and dial Natalie's number.

"Hey, Rox. Listen, I got your message

but I didn't get a chance to call you back till my shift was over."

"So, how was it?" I ask.

"Awesome! Well, it was totally exhausting, but it was so cool putting together killer outfits for people. I swear, one lady was almost moved to tears when I found the perfect dress for her ten-year high school reunion. It's great to feel so *needed*, you know?"

She rambles on for what seems like a week and finally stops to catch her breath. "Anyway, I'll shut up now, but I just can't tell you how much I appreciate you getting me this job. I'm still not sure how you did it, but I'm totally grateful."

"My pleasure, girl. I'm glad you're loving it."

"So how *did* you get me this job, Rox? I saw the stack of apps myself today. There had to be——"

"Zach and I broke up," I blurt out.

After a pause, she says, "Honey, I'm so sorry. Do you want me to bring some classics over? Maybe call Alex? We can pull an all-nighter like we used to. How about *Sixteen Candles* or *Pretty in Pink*?"

"That's okay. I'm really okay. . . ." I wonder what Alex is up to.

"How about some Ben and Jerry's?"

"No, no. I'm fine. It was totally mutual. Actually, if you really want to know the truth, I think he's back together with Eva."

"That's terrible! You'd think he'd learn his lesson about that beyotch. Her heart is tiny and black and shriveled up. Like a raisin or something."

I twirl open the blinds and then plop on my bed, stuffing a pillow under my chest. In the hallway I hear Dad reminding Chase to pack underwear for when he goes to Porter's. "She's really not that bad, Natalie. Besides, I think they're really good together."

From this angle, I have a clear view of the McCoy's house. Alex's Civic isn't there.

"So, tell me—does being a Siren agree with you?" I'm shocked Grandma Perkins said the S word in public, but a quick scan of the Dairy Queen reveals we're the only two souls in here, besides the freckle-faced twentysomething behind the counter. He's got headsets on, and he's drumming his hands on the cash register to the beat of whatever his iPod is blasting into his eardrums, impervious to our conversation.

"I notice you're driving your father's Porsche these days." Grandma Perkins winks at me, and then dunks the red plastic spoon into her vanilla malt. I called her an hour ago, asking her to meet me for a quick ice cream before she heads off to Jamaica. Or was it the Bahamas?

"I TiVo'd that fashion show you did at the mall, if you want to watch it sometime. You looked lovely, Roxy. I'm so proud of you."

"Oh, thanks." Did they happen to get coverage of my dainty little trip? I cram a bite of my milkshake into my mouth, the cold, minty, Oreo-chunky ice cream frolicking on my tongue.

Grandma licks her Liv Tyler lips and studies my face intently. "Are you still going with that boy from your school? The one you told me about?"

"No. That's so over."

"Oh, good." She relaxes her shoulders. "So you took my advice, I take it. . . ."

I shrug. "I guess so."

"Be careful, Roxy. I'd hate to see any harm come his way." Her green eyes darken.

I take another big bite of ice cream. With

my mouth full, I say, "You can't tell me you've never ever been in love, Grandma."

She blinks. "I most certainly have not. I'm a *Siren*."

"You made a baby with some guy. Weren't you in love with him? At least a little bit?"

She frowns. "I wanted a baby, that's all."

"So you slept with him till you got pregnant and once you got what you wanted, you left him. Is that your story?"

She opens her mouth as if to say something, then closes it. A moment later she says, "The point is, I wanted a baby and I got one. I love your mother very much. But I never loved her father. That's the way it has to be, Roxy. Because I'm a Siren." She reaches across the table and pats my hand. "And so are you."

"So you know, Mom's pretty pissed that you never told her anything about her father. Don't you think she has a right to know at least something about him?"

Grandma Perkins stares down at her lap. "I wish it could be different, but it can't. This is how it has to be."

I gaze out the window at the traffic-y

University Boulevard. It's getting dark outside, and most of the cars have their headlights on. "I was reading *The Siren Handbook* last night—"

"That's nice, honey. It's full of such wisdom."

"Do you really believe that if you fall in love with a man, he'll . . . die?"

"Yes, I do."

"How do you *know*? How do you know it's not just a part of the legend? We've never known another Siren, so maybe that part of *The Siren Handbook* is outdated. You know, like how Sirens are half-birds or mermaids or whatever."

She shakes her head, her eyes sad. "We must believe it word for word, Roxy. It's too great a risk to challenge it. Don't you remember what happened to the Siren called Thelxiepia?"

"She sang her Siren song and made a ship crash into the rocks by the island she lived on. Nothing new there, except that one of sailors miraculously made it to the shore alive. They fell in love and slept together and she got pregnant. But before the baby was born, the sailor died."

"She fell in love and her lover died. Don't you see? We can't have something like that on our consciences."

"So you left him before you could fall in love with him? Mom's father, I mean. To protect him?"

She breathes in and out, her perfect little nostrils flaring just a little. Then she sits up straight and performs her dazzling smile. "Did I tell you I'm going to Jamaica? This man I met has a lovely beach house, so I'm staying there."

"How do you know this guy?" I ask, perfectly aware that she changed the subject big-time.

She wipes her mouth with a napkin, taking her time. "I met him in a singles chat room, and then he took me to a delicious dinner at The Bistro on saxophone night. When he told me about his beach house, I showed an interest, and he gave me the key."

"When you were showing an interest, did you happen to break into song?"

"Well, dear, when I heard that saxophone, I just couldn't help singing along for a little while." Grandma Perkins stands up and tosses our empty cups and balled-up napkins into the trash can. The THANK YOU sign flaps back and forth. "Well, dear, I'd better get going. This was nice. We'll have to do it again."

I smile at her and say good-bye. Waving like a newly crowned beauty queen, she slips out the door and saunters to her Lexus. So graceful, so elegant, so perfect.

She may pretend to be having the time of her life, but I know better. She's sad and lonely, and I don't want to become like Grandma Perkins.

When I get home, Alex is leaning against my door in a white T-shirt, baggy shorts, and flip-flops. His sun-bleached hair glistens golden underneath the porch light. God, it's good to see him. I lean forward and hug him. We break our embrace and, inexplicably, I feel my face flush.

"Your mom wanted us to keep an eye on things while they're on vacation," he explains. "So I thought I'd drop by real quick and make sure everything's on the up-and-up."

Great. How many people does Mom have spying on me, anyway? "I assure you, I'm being a model daughter. Want to come in?" I ask, working my key in the door. The lock clicks and he follows me inside.

"I heard you helped Natalie get a job at that mall store," Alex says. "She's stoked. It's all she can talk about."

I shrug. "She was made for that job." I grab a couple of Cokes and meet him in the living room. He sprawls out on the couch and I plop down beside him.

"So, you're here to make sure I'm doing okay?" I click the stereo remote and Astra 8 It trickles through the speakers. I didn't even realize that Alex's favorite CD was still in there from when we were studying for our history final. "That was sweet of you."

"Yeah, well, that's me," Alex says. "Sweet as sugar." Though he's smiling, his eyes look cloudy.

I grab the afghan off the armrest and cuddle up with it. "I know I haven't been a very good friend lately. I haven't been a very good *person*. And you were right. I wasn't being real."

"You've changed a lot this summer, but . . ."

"But what?"

"Never mind." A minute later Alex says, "So, where did the 'rents go, anyway?"

"Disneyland. Guess they had a hankering to hang out with a freakishly large mouse in red trunks."

"Don't parents usually *take* their kids to Disney?"

I laugh. "I thought the same thing. Then again, my parents are a far cry from normal."

We sit in silence. Alex strums his fingers on his knee, in time to "Put Your Heart on Your Sleeve."

"So, have you played your trombone much this summer?" I ask, using the reserves in my small-talk vault.

"Nah. I'll probably be exiled to third seat once school starts up. Do you play your flute much?"

"A little." If he only knew . . .

"I saw Zach Parker at the movies last night. He and Eva were all over each other. So did you two break up, or do I have an ass-whoopin' to do?" He scrunches his face all up and smacks a fist into his open palm.

I crack up. "It's cool. We broke up. But it's not like we were ever serious or anything." Grandma Perkins would be so proud.

"So the wedding's off?" It looks like he's trying to maintain a straight face, but his lips keep twitching upward like he's got a tic. He shrugs. "Natalie told me you wanted to marry him."

I roll my eyes. She's so dead. "Yeah, well, that was when I was, like, twelve. Did she also mention I wanted to marry Orlando Bloom? And then adopt six kids from some third-world country?"

After Alex chuckles, he says, "I'm glad it's off."

"Why's that? You couldn't decide between the crystal bowl and the matching his-and-hers towel set?"

"No problem there. A Crock-Pot's the only way to go." He smiles. "Actually, I was scared you were going to ask me to be a bridesmaid. I'd feel so weird wearing a bridesmaid's gown next to Natalie. She has a much better figure than I do."

I whack him on the head with a pillow. "You're so weird. And for what it's worth, there's nothing wrong with your figure." Speaking of which, when did Alex go from a bony, awkward boy to a tanned, muscular guy?

He blows a flyaway hair off his face. "So, I suppose you're available now?"

"For what?" I reach in my pocket and

dangle my dad's car keys, jingling them in Alex's face. "A car pool?"

For a moment he watches the keys like a cat playing with string. Then he grabs my hand and holds it still in midair. "You know what I mean. Why do you always turn everything into a joke? I'm trying to level with you here, and you're making it so . . . difficult," he says, squeezing my hand with an intensity that makes my stomach flip-flop.

I reel in my grin and put the keys on the coffee table. "Sorry. You were saying . . . ?"

He releases my hand and then runs his finger around a button on the couch. "I'm curious. Did you ever read what I wrote in your yearbook?"

"Yeah, sure." Truth is, I don't remember if I read it or not. But I'm not going to hurt his feelings by admitting that. I do recall him keeping my yearbook for four whole periods while he wrote it in. Not that it was a big deal. It's not like I had hundreds of people lined up to autograph my yearbook.

"And . . . ?"

"Uh, it was very . . . nice," I say.

He nods, looking into my eyes as if he's trying to read a deeper meaning. Without any warning, he leans even closer and kisses me full on the mouth. I close my eyes and kiss him back for a second, and then pull back with a jolt.

I spring up off the couch. "What? What are you doing?" My lips are tingling, my eyes are stinging, and I can't decide whether to run out of the room or dive into his arms.

He stands and reaches for my hand, but I don't give it to him. "I'm just . . . I just wanted to kiss you."

"Don't."

"Why not, Roxy? Why the hell not? Give me one good reason. Just tell me—you know, so I can get you out of my system."

I feel my jaw slacken, but the words won't come. They're hidden somewhere in the depths of my throat.

Alex stares at me, waiting. But when I don't answer him, he just shoves his hands in his pockets and makes a beeline for the door.

I run to the window. As Alex jogs down the street, it's like the floor is quicksand and I'm sinking lower and lower. I drop to my knees and stare as he disappears into the night. Astra 8 It croons in the living room, bringing back memories of going to their concerts. With Alex. Adorable, nice Alex.

"Please don't go, Alex." My voice sounds so small in the empty house. "I just don't want to screw everything up."

Am I too late? Have I already screwed it all up?

The CD ends and the stereo turns itself off. The house has never been so quiet. I lug myself up and run to my bedroom. What did Alex write in my yearbook?

Fifteen

Bingo. Under the bed.

I flip through the pages of the yearbook, most of which feature sports, student government, and anything else the Proud Crowd is into. Turning to the back, I scope out the band pictures. We're all holding our instruments like they're our babies. This is the page Natalie chose to sign:

Hiya, Alex,
Thank you for being in band. Without you, people
would be making fun of me for being the worst—

Whoa. Rewind.
Alex? I flip through a few more pages

and realize that somehow I've got Alex's yearbook. So if this one is Alex's, he must have mine. Wonderful. Now he's going to know I lied about having read what he wrote.

I flick through his yearbook until I spot the page with my handwriting on it. It's next to my photo.

It's a good thing the Sea Nymph gene found its way into my chromosomes. Imagine going through life looking like *that*. Strange, but I thought I looked pretty decent that day. I mean, I never equated myself to Lindsay Lohan or anything quite that delusional. Well, maybe . . . if Lindsay never worked out, wore Coke-bottle glasses, shopped Target's clearance racks, and had pimples and frizzy hair. I'd written in loopy, turquoise letters:

Hey, Alex,
I'll never forget our crazy times together. Remember when we put Saran Wrap on the toilet in Mr. Ziggler's bathroom at band camp? He got so pissed (literally)! And remember when I wrote a note on your mom's letterhead, explaining that you get horrible migraines, so

you could leave any class at any time without
question? LOL. Anyway, this summer's gonna
rock. See ya at Murphy's!
Love ya,
xoxo
Roxy

I'm laughing out loud, the memories
flooding my mind. We really have had some
good times together, Alex and me.

The next morning, I grab Alex's yearbook,
jump in the Boxster, and zip down to his
house. His mom answers the door, her
peroxide-blond hair a beehive of rollers.
"Roxy? Is that you? Land sakes, you've sure
blossomed." She touches her hair, looking
kinda self-conscious.

"Thanks, Patricia. Is Alex around?"

"Come on in, dear. So, I hear your parents went to California?"

"Yeah. They're celebrating their anniversary."

She stands there in the foyer, staring at me
like I'm a Girl Scout and she's trying to
decide how many boxes of Thin Mints to buy.

"Is Alex here?" I ask again.

She shakes her head, looking decades

older than Grandma Perkins. "He's at work at the car wash."

This must be my lucky day! Maybe I can switch the yearbooks and Alex will be none the wiser. I'd already planned to tell him the truth, that I hadn't read what he'd written. It would've been difficult, especially since he's not exactly happy with me right now, but I felt it was the right thing to do. I don't want to make the same mistake I made with Natalie. But now, since he's not home . . .

Patricia says, "Is everything okay, Roxy? You look a little—"

"I think I might have left something in his room. Do you mind if I go back and look for it?"

"Not at all. Help yourself. I'll just be in my office."

"Okay, thanks." I wander up to his bedroom and flip on the light. It's tidy, but nowhere as clean as mine is these days, thanks to my little bro's maid service. He's got three Ansel Adams photos on the wall, and a *Pirates of the Caribbean* movie poster that I gave him ages ago. A potted cactus rests on the window ledge, and a collection of bobblehead dolls adorns his dresser.

I open his squeaky closet door and rummage around, searching for my yearbook. Finally, I spot it on the top shelf, behind his trombone case.

Flopping onto the navy plaid quilt on his bed, I open the book to the band photo pages. I instantly recognize Alex's miniature, scratchy print:

Hey, Rox,
It's been cool going to school with you all these years. I remember being in band together in the fifth grade, right after I moved here. You were the first person I met in Colorado. (Well, besides the real estate agent. And that lady who lives across the street with all the gnomes in her yard.) You turned around and smiled at me, even though I couldn't make a decent noise out of my trombone. Then you told me to stick with it when I wanted to quit, sometime during our eighth-grade year. Now here we are, just two more years of high school (yay!), and I couldn't have made it without you.
See ya,
Alex

Hmm. Sweet, but I have to admit I was expecting something more . . . I don't know, profound? I mean, he made such a big deal out of my reading it. And then, when he kissed me, well, I thought maybe he'd written something about . . . well, never mind.

Alex kissed me. That was totally bizarre. But was it, really? Or was it kind of . . . nice?

I glance over the faces of my fellow band geeks, briefly recalling our times in summer camps and our competitions with the other high schools in Boulder and the Springs. And when I spot a blond-haired wisp of a boy grasping a trombone with both hands, I smile to myself. The guy who always stared at me and wanted to bet which song we were going to play for the concert finale. He brought Skittles to band almost every day, sharing with me. My flute always smelled fruity, thanks to Alex.

Alex McCoy was the boy I wished I could just stuff into my locker whenever Zach Parker and the other jocks passed by us in the halls. I was ashamed of Alex. I was embarrassed to be his friend whenever any of the Proud Crowd group was around, like when Eva and Amber were at 7-Eleven. As these revelations hit me, I feel like I just ate a handful of Sour Patch Kids with a mouthful of canker sores. The sour, stinging, painful truth.

I turn to the little black-and-white sophomore class pictures and find Alex's. Next to his photograph, in black chicken scratch print, are the words *"I love you. A.M."*

I feel a weird, fluttery sensation somewhere behind my rib cage. It's barely noticeable at first, and then it grows more and more intense. Slowly, I lower my head onto his pale yellow pillow.

Sure, I pretty much knew that Alex had a crush on me. But do I like him back . . . like that? I've been so obsessed with getting Zach Parker to notice me, have I brushed off my true feelings for Alex?

What's that smell? I take a small whiff, and next, a bigger one. Then I bury my nose in his pillowcase. It smells delicious. Speed Stick–Irish Spring delicious. Alex McCoy delicious. I could lie here breathing in his signature scent forever.

After snapping the yearbook shut, I place his on the top shelf of the closet and turn out the light. My book tucked under my arm, I roam down the hall and poke my head into Patricia's office. She's a freelance journalist, and with all her newspapers, magazines, and who-knows-what-else, her workspace is a freaking disaster area. I'm serious. Someday somebody's going to call Disaster Cleanup or that reality TV show where those two ladies miraculously organize everything. But until then, I'll just be mindful of stepping around the piles.

Patricia swivels around in her mustard yellow office chair, knocking over a mug of coffee. Thank God, it's nearly empty. "Hi, Roxy. Did you find what you were looking for?" She sops up the small black puddle with the bottom of her Reebok sweatshirt.

"I did. Thanks."

I pull into the parking lot at Liberty Park. Today I'm doing that photo shoot for Vail's upcoming hot-air balloon fest, and, luckily, it's another of Colorado's bluebird-blue sky days. There's a makeshift makeup and wardrobe area set up in the little white gazebo. Three men are dragging a hot-air balloon basket this way, and a group of little kids are following them Pied Piper—style across the lawn.

"Yoo-hoo! Are you Roxy Zimmerman?" a voluptuous woman hollers from inside the gazebo.

"That's me."

"Oh, good. I'm Mac Baxter, and I'm going to be doing your makeup today." She holds my hand as I take a seat on an old-time barstool.

A hobbitlike man jumps into the gazebo and says, "I'm making a Starbucks run. Would you ladies like anything?"

"Aren't you an angel!" Mac says. "I'll take a coffee—black—and a scone."

"I'd love a vanilla latte," I say, and the little man takes off across the park.

A changing curtain is set up in the opposite corner of the gazebo, and an elegant black ball gown hangs from a lattice. "You're a pretty young lady," Mac says, wrapping a makeup bib around my neck to protect my track jacket. "Just look at that skin. It's positively flawless! And I don't think I've ever seen such green eyes." In a frenzy of foundation, eyeliner, mascara, powder, lip liner, and lipstick, she dots, sponges, smears, swishes, brushes, and blends. She pauses, makeup sponge midair, and catches my eye in the mirror. "What's wrong, dear?"

"How do you know if it's love, Mac?"

Before she can answer, the production

assistant sets my grande Starbucks cup on the counter, next to the case of eye shadows. He's breathing heavily, as if he's been running. I take a sip. "Thanks, I needed this."

Apparently satisfied, our personal barista exits, his Vans smacking the asphalt path as he hurries off to assist the photographer.

I twirl the Starbucks cup around and around on my knee. What's this? I pick it up and study the logo more closely. I jump in my seat, eyeliner streaking from my eyelid to ear.

Could it be?

"Oh, dear. I'm so sorry. . . ."

It's a Siren! There's a picture of a Siren, right here on my coffee cup.

"Let me get a tissue. . . ."

How many hundreds of Starbucks cups have I drunk out of in my lifetime, and why am I just now seeing the Siren?

The way the sunlight dapples through the lattices, the Siren's eyes seem to glow. Is she trying to tell me something?

I wait, but nothing happens.

Mac dabs at my right eye, looking at me with one finely plucked eyebrow arched. "You're staring at that like you've never seen a coffee cup before. Are you sure you're okay?"

Then it dawns on me. Sirens don't sit on their butts waiting for something to happen. They *make* it happen!

"Actually, I'm not okay. I messed up. But I'm going to be okay. I just need to talk to somebody. I need to go. I'm sorry." I stand up start running through the park.

"Wait! Only one eye is done!"

After hitting a gas station and stocking up on Skittles, I drive the Boxster over to the car wash. I walk into the little office, and three guys in Auto Spa T-shirts stop what they're doing to check me out. (Will I ever get used to that?)

A guy with a Sudoku puzzle in his lap says, "Hello, young lady. You looking for an application?"

Ignoring him, I close the door behind me. "Where is Alex McCoy working today?" I ask the older man, who to me looks the most "managerish." His name tag reads STANLEY.

"Um, yeah. Do you want me to get him for you?" Stanley asks, sitting up straighter in his folding chair.

The fan on a little table hums softly, puffing and wheezing in a gallant effort to cool the room. A gust promptly catches my hair, and I feel it lift and then fall back into place, every strand picture-perfect. "No. Actually, I just need to know which part of the car wash he's working today."

"He's waxing, under the blue tent," the Sudoku guy offers, flashing his toothy grin.

"Thanks." Hmm. "Who actually drives the cars from the exterior wash to the waxing tent?"

Stanley nods toward the window. "Missy's doing that."

I whip out my flute and play until Stanley is fully under my Siren powers. "Stanley, go tell Missy and Alex to switch." I look at the rest of the guys in the room (who are also under the spell, natch) and say, "And don't mention me to anybody."

"Sure thing." With that, Stanley jogs out the side door and I hurry back to the Boxster to get everything ready. Then I sit on a bench in the shade and watch Alex drive a Buick, a Nissan, and finally a red Porsche Boxster to the tent. A few minutes later he steps out of the Boxster and looks around. Then he spots me sitting here and runs over, his smile reaching from ear to ear.

"Roxy!"

"Hey, Alex." I stand up and he gives me one of his fabulous hugs.

"You mean it?"

"Of course I mean it, you big goof! What are you waiting for?"

I lean closer to him, catching a whiff of that delicious Speed Stick–Irish Spring cocktail that I've been craving. And then I kiss him right on the mouth. It's absolutely, spontaneously, romantically perfect. My head spinning, my knees wobbly, I sink onto the bench.

Alex rakes his fingers through his blond hair, giving it a good dose of I-don't-give-a-shit-what-my-hair-looks-like. He sits next to me, fixes me with his puppy-dog eyes, and says, "So, is this a tribute to *Clockwork Orange*?"

I wrinkle my nose. "What are you talking about?"

"Your makeup. It's caked onto this eye"— he lightly touches my left temple—"and this one has no makeup at all." Now he touches my right temple, sending a zing of electricity from my head through my entire body.

"And what's this? I've never been into cutting-edge fashion, but what's this supposed to be? The bib look?"

Oh, God. I reach up to my neck, and sure enough, I'm still wearing the paper clothes-shield thingie. How embarrassing! I rip it off and stuff it into my tote. "Better?"

He shrugs. "Whatever makes you happy."

You make me happy. That's what I want to say. I feel like I'm going to explode, I want to say it so badly.

"Did you really come out here to kiss me?"

"No." I rest my head on his shoulder. "I came here to apologize for lying to you. I said I read what you wrote in my yearbook, but I hadn't. But now I *have* read it, and . . ." Ugh. This isn't coming out like I'd hoped.

He takes my hand and asks, "Wanna blow this joint?"

"Why, Alex! Are you saying you're going to ditch work?"

"I just happen to have an excellent excuse this time."

"Oh?"

He says, "Yeah, migraine," and I crack up. He springs off the bench and helps me up.

"Let's go."

I look around for my car. "Have you seen an adorable red Boxster lying around?"

"Apparently, the owner only wanted an

exterior wash and wax, but when I was driving it out of the car wash, I noticed that the words KISS ME were spelled out in Skittles across the front seat. So it was my professional opinion that the car had to be vacuumed. Of course, at no added expense to the customer. After all, at Auto Spa, we aim to please."

I drawl in a fake Southern accent, "Why, Alex. That's mighty sweet of you," and give him another kiss.

"That's me, sweet as sugar."

Sixteen

*The next morn, Thelxiepia discovered
a lone, shipwrecked sailor sleeping
beneath an olive tree. He protected her
as her older sisters had done, and, lying
on a bed of flowers, Thelxiepia confessed
her love to the sailor.*

I'm totally psyched to have the house to
myself 'cause Alex and I decided that for
our first official date, we'd just hang out
here.

We order a Hawaiian pizza and Cheese-
Bread from Blackjack Pizza and then watch
Pirates of the Caribbean snuggled on the couch
in pillows and blankets. We talk and talk and
talk. And then we somehow get into this

crazy pillow fight. I can't tell you who kisses whom first. It just happens. When we come up for air, I pluck a feather off Alex's nose and kiss it. His nose, not the feather.

Suddenly he pushes me away. "How come you wouldn't kiss me last night, but you're all into it today? What's changed?"

"*I've* changed, Alex."

He springs up and stalks into the kitchen. I follow, sidestepping Pumpkin.

"So, *how* have you changed?" Alex asks, grabbing a couple of Cokes out of the fridge.

I twirl a strand of my silky hair, thinking.

"I mean, despite the obvious," he adds, unwrapping my hair from my finger and looking into my emerald green eyes.

"Are you really going to make me go into a speech about not judging people and being honest . . . all that deep stuff?"

He shakes his head and briefly presses his finger on my lips. "It's late. I should probably give my mom a call. You know, let her know where I am and all that."

"Do you want to stay over? You know, like the good ol' days?"

He gives me a tiny grin and I notice his cheeks are flushed. "Sure."

Five minutes later I turn off the light in my bedroom. As I'm drifting off to sleep, tucked seamlessly against Alex's side, I feel more comfortable than I've ever felt. I bask in his warmth, his scent, the mesmerizing sound of his heartbeat. Am I just dreaming, or did he really kiss me lightly on the forehead and whisper, "I love you, Roxy Zimmerman"?

When the sun blasts through the window the next morning, Alex kisses me on the lips.

We lie here like this for an hour, talking some of the time about everyday things. Other times, saying nothing at all, listening to each other breathe. It's during one of the quiet times that my stomach decides to let out a superloud growl.

"Guess that's my cue to get crackin' on breakfast," he says, running his fingertips up and down my back. "It's the least I can do, after that gourmet meal you spent hours on last night."

I laugh. Without a trace of grace, he rolls off the bed and stumbles to get his footing. I watch as he pulls a pair of tan shorts over his adorable Superman boxers. "I'll be back in a flash. You just stay here and hold down the fort." He puts on his Auto Spa shirt and then disappears down the hall. I hear him fumbling with the deadbolt on the front door.

I run after him, down the hall. I just assumed we'd have Pop-Tarts or cereal. "Where are you going?"

He flips around, his hair bearing a striking resemblance to a troll doll's. "McDonald's. You know, home of the Egg McMuffin?"

"Mmmm. My favorite."

"I know." He smiles at me as I pry open the lock. Then he goes out the front door, closing it softly behind him.

I watch him jog to his Civic. What's happening? My body is alternating between hot flashes and chills. I swing the door open and run out onto the lawn. "Alex, wait!"

I really shouldn't. What if the Siren curse is for real? But if it's so wrong for me to feel this way, why does it feel so *right*?

Oh, God. I feel like I'm about to explode. Here it comes. "I . . . really-think-I'm-falling-in-love-with-you."

He cracks a grin. He's going to laugh at me. He's going to freak out. He's going to . . . sprint over to me and give me a rib-crushing hug.

I feel his heart banging against my chest as we cleave to each other. Alex stoops down and rests his forehead on mine. "You have no idea how happy that makes me."

I kiss him gently and then pat his butt and send him on his way to McDonald's for the yummiest breakfast in the world.

Half an hour passes.

Even if the traffic is horrendous, Alex should be back by now. I pick up the cordless phone and dial his cell number. It goes directly into his "Either I'm too busy to pick up or I'm screening my calls and you didn't make the cut" voice mail message. He should probably add "or my battery isn't charged," because I'm sure that's why he's not answering.

After I throw away the Blackjack box and toss the pop cans in the recycle bin, I flick on the TV. Nothing's on. I put in the DVD we watched last night. I can't seem to concentrate. I pick up the *Gossip Girl* book that Natalie lent me, but the words are just a big black blur.

I'm bored.

I call Natalie. "Hey, girl. What's up?" she answers.

"Just hanging out with Alex. But he

went to get some food and hasn't come back. He's not over there, is he?"

"Haven't seen him. But I'll let you know if I do, okay? Gotta run, talk soon!" She makes a kissy noise and then the line goes dead.

I hang up and stare at the phone.

Which McDonald's did Alex go to, the one in Steamboat Springs?

After an hour, I'm seriously worried. "Where the hell is he?" I say out loud. I flip on the stereo and try to relax with The Ataris. But it doesn't work. I begin imagining the worst.

I scared him. That's the only thing that makes sense. I shouldn't have confessed my feelings for him. It was one thing for him to have a thing for me, but it probably freaked him out when I told him I felt the same way. We've always been friends. Now we're friends who hooked up. It happens all the time. I should've kept love out of it. Why'd I have to go and make everything so complicated?

Then a horrible thought slithers into my skull. What if . . . ? No. There's no way Alex is dead. *The Siren Handbook* can't be serious about the If-you-fall-in-love-with-someone-he'll-die rule. *The Siren Handbook* is so old—archaic, even. It's just a bunch of mythical mumbo jumbo.

Sure, a long time ago the men whom Sirens loved probably died. But back then, a twenty-three-year-old could collect Social Security and get the senior discount at the movies. There were all sorts of diseases and plagues and battles and cliffs without guardrails. Dog bite? Sorry, you're going to die. Poison ivy? Definitely doomed. Bad hair day? You're history, baby.

I run into my room and flip through *The Siren Handbook*. You can't take every word literally. Look at this: "If a Siren allows a man to get too close to her, he will die." The Sirens back then lived on an island surrounded by deadly rocks. So, obviously if a man got too "close" to a Siren, he'd die. He'd smash into the rocks and die.

It's kind of weird how Grandma Perkins is so adamant about not falling in love with a man, though. Kind of scary, too. Very scary. I grab my purse, jump into the meticulously clean Boxster, and speed out of the neighborhood. If I have to look at every pair of golden arches in this whole freaking state, I'm going to find Alex.

The first McDonald's I come to is surrounded by fire trucks, cop cars, and an ambulance. I can't breathe and I don't think my heart is beating.

Like a wounded soldier, Alex's Civic lies on its side in a ditch. A little red cinnamon-apple-scented tree pokes out of the dirt by the front tire. My knees are so wobbly and my hands are shaking so violently, I have the hardest time driving to the side of the road. Oh, God. There's a huge semi half a block up in the ditch, facing the opposite direction. My skin is prickling like I just wallowed in stinging nettle.

I grab my flute and run to the nearest policeman. "What happened?"

"Car wreck," he mutters, not even looking up from his computer-thingie. I don't have time for him to be all vague. I whip out my flute and play, ripping his sunglasses off his face so I can see his eyes. When he's under my Siren powers, I say, "Tell me everything you know about what happened here."

"A young man, identified by his driver's license to be Alexander McCoy, age sixteen, was coming out of the McDonald's drive-through in his Honda Civic, when he broadsided that semi over yonder, which was exceeding the speed limit by a good twenty miles per hour. The truck driver is fine, but the McCoy kid was rushed to St. Mary's Hospital. Terrible."

Oh my God! Poor Alex! I've got to get to him.

"Alex McCoy. Is he okay?" I shout at the first person I see in the ER: an elderly, blue-haired volunteer in a Monet-inspired pinafore. She clicks her tongue and positions herself in front of a computer, striking keys in shaky slow-motion.

"Let's see . . . car accident. Oh, my. Yes, he's here."

"Can I see him?"

She adjusts her glasses and then focuses on me. "I'm sorry, but he's in critical condition. They've taken him straight to surgery."

"What do you mean?" At least he's not dead. I mean, I highly doubt they operate on people when they're already dead. I swipe away my tears, knowing that if I start crying, I won't be able to stop. "The doctors are doing everything they can," she says in her quiet, baritone voice. "You can sit in the waiting room, if you like."

The requisite fish tank, scratchy chairs, and weak magazine selection welcome me in the waiting room. As I sit here, I'm fit to be tied. Or sent to the loony bin, at least.

He's going to die. I killed Alex by falling in love with him. I'm sure my bawling, screaming, flailing of arms, and stomping of feet distresses everyone around me, but I don't care. I shake my head and pace around. Then I sit down on the coffee table and throw a pile of *Newsweek* and *Parenthood* magazines on the orange carpet.

"Miss? Please don't do that," the old lady in Monet says.

I pick up one of the magazines and hurl it at the TV, right as one of the *Young and the Restless* stars screams, "You killed my baby!"

With shaking hands, I reach into my tote for my cell. When my fingers graze my flute, it feels warm, like I've been playing it in a full-length concert. I pull out the phone and dial Grandma Perkins.

Oh no. I can't hold the sobs back a second longer. "I've made a horrible mistake, Grandma. A horrible, deadly mistake."

After a slight pause, she asks, "What have you done, dear? I'm sure it's not as bad as you think."

I collapse into one of the rock-hard chairs and bury my face in my free hand. "I think I fell in love."

Silence. "With that football player you were seeing? But I thought—"

"No, Alex McCoy. We're in band and a bunch of classes together. We've been good friends forever. But something strange happened. Something changed. It's like everything we've ever done together, everything we've ever said to each other, took on a whole new life. There was no warning—"

"There never is. That's why love is so dangerous. Have you told him?"

"Told him what?"

"That you're in love with him?"

"Yes." A fresh batch of tears trails down my cheeks. "And he got in a car accident and he's at the hospital. He's in critical condition, Grandma." Oh, God. What have I done? I'm a murderer! I'm no better than those Sirens in Greek myths who lured mariners to their deaths with their sweet music and beautiful faces.

I hear her ragged breathing through the phone. "Well, what's done is done. I'm afraid we're just going to have to let it run its course."

"But I don't want him to die! Isn't there something I can do? Can I use my Siren powers to fix it? Can I play my flute and have the doctors make him good as new?"

"It doesn't work that way, Roxy. You can't make someone do something they're incapable of doing. The doctors will do the best they can, whether you use your Siren powers on them or not."

"Isn't there anything in *The Siren Handbook* that'll help? Like an elixir or a special spell or something?" I'd read the book cover to cover, but I figure asking wouldn't hurt. You know, in case I missed it somehow.

She whispers, "No." Just as I expected. Just as I feared.

"They won't even let me in to see him. I have to wait in this putrid waiting room. Oh, God. What if he dies all alone? I've got to get in there to see him!"

"Use your Siren powers, Roxy. Go to him. I'll be there as soon as I can."

I hang up the phone and pull out my flute. There are a few men in the waiting room, a middle-aged cowboy, a pudgy guy wearing a Pi Kappa Alpha baseball cap, and a man who looks like he hasn't showered in a week. I lift the flute to my lips and play the best I can with tears flowing down my face. When the men are swaying and completely at the mercy of the Siren song, I put the flute back in my bag. "Distract the old lady. I'm going in."

They circle around the hospital volunteer, and the college dude tells her that her hair is so sexy and it reminds him of Marge Simpson. I'm not so sure that's a compliment, but by the flush on her cheeks, I'd say she's flattered. I wait until she's completely immersed in their attentions. Then I sneak past the desk and fly down the hall in search of Alex.

People in white jackets and robin's-egg blue scrubs whiz by me, paying no attention to the redheaded band nerd who masquerades as a beautiful Siren. I peek into all the rooms, finally finding Alex in the farthest one. At least, I *think* it's Alex.

I feel as if my stomach is slithering down my body and splatting on the bluish-white linoleum.

There's an oxygen mask over Alex's mouth. His eyes are closed, as if he's asleep. Everything about him appears corpselike and red and unreal. Like a character out of a Tim Burton movie.

A male doctor and two nurses (one male, one female) are buzzing around the bed, speaking in indecipherable medical language. "Possible spleenectomy . . . exploration of abdomen . . . closures of lacerations . . ."

Alex's shorts and gray Auto Spa shirt (now cut up) are lying on the countertop, beside some syringes and bandages and tubes of some sort.

I step inside the fluorescent-lit room. The doctor and nurses look up at me, shocked. Before they have a chance to ask me who I am and what I think I'm doing, I blow a series of half-hearted puffs into my flute. Then I say, "Tell me what's happening."

"She can't be in here, doctor," a nurse mutters.

The doctor turns his attention back to his patient, pressing his stethoscope to Alex's chest. As he starts listing all the horrific injuries, my stomach lurches. Oh. My. God. Poor Alex.

I take a deep breath, the stench of blood and alcohol mixing in my nostrils. "Is he going to . . . die?"

The doctor looks up at me and smiles. For an instant I assume he's going to tell me that Alex is fine. That he'll be good as new in a week or two. So when the words "It doesn't look good" tear through my ears and crash into my brain, I shake my head in disbelief. The more I shake it, the blurrier my vision gets. I feel hands on my shoulders, steering me out of the room and into the darkness.

Seventeen

As her lover took his final breaths, the young Siren took the sailor's head in her palms and lamented, "Dear lover, I must confess that I am a Siren and I alone have brought this fate upon you."

The next morn, the sailor lay lifeless and cold, his handsome face moist from the tears of Thelxiepia, now a plain maiden.

"I came as soon as I could get here, honey," Grandma Perkins's voice rings from somewhere far away. I lift my eyelids and her suntanned face comes slowly into focus. "Let's get you something to eat, to get your strength back up."

I don't think I can eat a single morsel of food, especially hospital cafeteria food, but I take her hand and amble down the long, brightly lit hallway. I sit down in the closest booth while Grandma grabs a tray.

Patricia McCoy is in the cafeteria, chugging coffee like she has the inside scoop on an impending coffee bean shortage. Running over to her, I give her a hug and kiss her tear-stained cheek. I can't think of anything to say. What do you say to the mother of your murder victim? Her eyes are puffy from crying, her hair haywire, and her clothes wrinkled. Her ashen face tells me that the doctor's words still hold true. That it doesn't look good.

She hugs me, her entire body convulsing into sobs. In a tiny, distant voice, she says, "They asked me if he's a donor."

Oh, God. "I'm sure they ask that whenever anyone goes into surgery, Patricia. It's probably protocol, that's all." My voice sounds strangely calm.

"Maybe he'll wake up soon." She tells me which ICU room he's in. I flag down my grandmother and tell her I'll be right back.

The longer I walk, the farther the hall seems to stretch. I pass room numbers 1172,

1174, 1176, and finally stop in front of room number 1178. I've run out of gas. I can't go on.

The door opens, revealing a curvaceous nurse in turquoise and pink swirled scrubs. There's a pen stuck behind her ear and a plastic clipboard tucked under her arm. "Are you one of Alex's sisters?"

I nod, just in case they won't let a non-relative in, and she steps out of my way. "He's in an induced coma," she says. "Go ahead and talk to him, though. It never hurts."

Oh my God! No! "He's in a coma?"

"An induced coma, dear. Didn't your mom tell you?"

Mom? Oh, right. Patricia. "You mean you *induced* a coma? You put him in a coma? On purpose?"

"Yes. It's actually a fairly common practice. Your brother would be in a lot of pain otherwise. Plus he's on a ventilator, and putting him in a coma keeps him from pulling out the tubes. It's for his own good, really."

But you have no idea what's happening, I want to yell. *You have no idea that I'm a Siren and I told him I love him and he's going to die, and putting him in a freaking coma just makes it that much worse. Because, because . . . well, he looks like he's dead already!*

She leaves, quietly closing the door behind her.

My breath catches in my throat. I inch over to the bed. His skin looks puffy and dull, and judging by all the little bandages and bruises on his arms, he's been a virtual pincushion. I bend over and kiss him softly on the forehead, and then brush my lips across his cold, clammy cheek. "Dear God, what have I done?" I whisper.

The only response I get is the humming of the medical machines.

I take his hand and stare at his closed eyelids. "This is all my fault, Alex. All my fault." I wipe a wayward tear before it drips down onto his swollen face.

I rise and wander over to the window. Dark clouds clump in the sky, creating ominous shadows on the street. The cars look so tiny from up here, the trees like sprigs of broccoli. Even the mountains appear small and insignificant.

"You see, Alex, I messed up. I shouldn't have let myself fall in love with you. If I'd listened to my grandma, and if I'd taken *The Siren Handbook* seriously, you wouldn't be here."

I return to his bedside, sit down in the chair, and scoot it as close to Alex as it'll go. Smoothing his hair, I ask, "Why am I so stupid?" I wait, in case he feels like answering, but of course, he's just lying there in his coma.

A moment later his little finger twitches. Is it just my imagination, or did his left eyelid just flutter? I know I should call the nurse, get someone in here. But I'm glued to the chair. I want to be here when he wakes up. I want to be the first person he sees.

"Please wake up, Alex. Please be okay."

Nothing.

"I have something to tell you. Something very important. I don't know if you're going to believe me, and I don't blame you if you think I've gone off the deep end. But I have to let you know." I take a deep breath and watch his face for any sign of life. But he's a statue. "You're always telling me to be honest with you, Alex, and now I'm going to. It's the least I can do."

I have to swallow several times before I can speak another word. Leaning closer, I whisper into his ear, "I am a Siren. I'm a Siren and I can make men do anything I want. That's how I got Zach Parker to date me. Not that I'm proud of that. But it's true. I used my Siren powers to become a model. I even got my dad to relinquish the keys to his beloved Boxster with my Siren powers. You know what? I never even took my driver's test. I used my Siren powers on the driving instructor, and he passed me for just driving around the parking lot a couple of times.

"You see, everything I've gotten, everything I've achieved this summer, I owe to being a Siren. And one of the rules about being a Siren is you can't fall in love. I broke that rule, Alex. I broke it horribly. The car wreck wasn't your fault. It was mine."

Every muscle in my body aches, and my head pounds wickedly. I feel like I've eaten a whole stack of saltines with no water to wash them down. But at least I'm alive.

Alex is in a coma. If *The Siren Handbook* is right about his fate, he's going to die. I wish I could die instead.

A high-pitched buzz fills the air, and bodies dressed in scrubs flood into the room. "You have to leave, miss," a voice says, guiding me out of the way and shutting the door in my face.

When I open my eyes, it takes me a while to get my bearings. I'm curled up in a ball on the orange carpet of the waiting room. Grandma Perkins is looking down at me, a concerned look on her blurry face.

Then I remember. Alex. Alex was in a deadly car wreck because of me. My body jolts as if I'd just been shocked by a defibrillator. "How is he? How is Alex? Is he . . . alive?"

"You told him."

I groan, trying to sit up. I can't believe I fell asleep at a time like this, but something's not right with my body. "What, that I love him? I already told you that." I can hardly move, and my muscles are throbbing like crazy.

"No, what I mean is, you told him you're a Siren."

"Tell me how he is. How's Alex?"

She sighs and takes my hands, helping me to my feet. "You've managed to break both rules."

"I'm sure Alex isn't going to tell the evil

scientists about us." My eyes brim with hot tears. "Hel-*lo*? He's in a freaking coma!" I reach for a tissue and wipe my nose. "So what if I told Alex my secret? Now I'm not going to be a Siren anymore?"

"Roxy, listen to me. We've got to leave. I know you want to stay here with Alex, but you've got to trust me. Please. Come with me," she says, reaching out her hand.

I hesitate, but the look in Grandma Perkins's eyes is so scary-intense, I do as she says. I take her hand and walk out of the hospital, not looking back.

It's dark outside, and I'm shocked to see that it's well past eleven o'clock. As Grandma whizzes along in her Lexus, the streetlights cast eerie shadows on her face. She reaches over and turns off her satellite radio, the low hum of tires on concrete the only sound.

I blink over and over again. Even though her car is as spotlessly clean as always, it's like the windshield is coated with an inch of Vaseline. I rub my eyes, but it doesn't help. The entire world is blurry.

I reach my hand up to my head and touch my hair. It's frizzy and tangled. I peer down at my chest and see that my boobs have deflated. I'm Plain Jane again. Just a band geek. A part of me feared this would happen. If *The Siren Handbook* was right about Rule Number Two, it was probably right about Rule Number One.

Grandma breaks at a red light and turns to me. She opens her mouth as if to say something, but then promptly snaps it shut.

"Is Alex *alive*?" I almost scream, staring into my grandma's piercing green eyes.

"Apparently, he's doing quite well, considering."

"Is he awake? Did he wake up from the coma?"

She nods, a small smile on her pretty lips.

"So why did you take me away from the hospital? Why didn't you let me see him?" The light turns green and she hits the gas. Otherwise, I just might be jumping out of this car and footing it back to St. Mary's Hospital.

"Well, first of all, Alex can't have visitors till the morning. It doesn't do anyone any good to spend the night in that waiting room when there's a perfectly good bed at your house. Second of all, we need to talk, Roxy. In complete privacy." She swivels her head right and left, as if making sure there aren't any mini-spies suction-cupped to the windows. "When we were at Dairy Queen, you said some things that have been lingering in my mind. Haunting me, even. My mother, your great-grandmother, was adamant about following the Siren Rules, and I accepted them with blind faith. It never occurred to me to question the Rules, as you were doing. It never occurred to me that perhaps an element of the equation was missing, something right before our very eyes. How could something be so small that thousands of Sirens had overlooked it, yet at the same time, so enormous that it would change the lives of all Sirens today and yet to be born?"

Grandma blinks slowly, reverently, before continuing. "I need to ask you an important question, Roxy. So take your time answering. Now think back and tell me this: Did you ever use your Siren powers on Alex?"

I rack my brains, but I can't recall ever playing my flute for Alex. Not a single time. I guess I could've chosen to play it when he was working at Auto Spa and I had the Boxster washed and waxed for free. Or when he was working at the theater and got me into all the movies without a ticket. But I didn't. And his kiss was amazing without my having to seek mystical help. "No, I never did."

Now she's grinning from ear to ear, and her words are coming faster and faster. "You see, the Siren named Thelxiepia fell in love with a sailor and he died. That's the legend that's been passed down generation after generation. But there's one part of the story that we've taken for granted. Thelxiepia's lover was *under her Siren spell*. She'd sung to him when he was on his ship and drew him in, just like all the other sailors who'd heard the song of the Siren over the course of time."

"So you're saying that because I never used my Siren powers on Alex . . ."

". . . you didn't cause the car wreck," Grandma finishes for me.

"I didn't cause the wreck!" As this is sinking in, I feel a deep, satisfying sense of peace. All the fear and tension lifts out of my body and dissolves into the air.

Grandma Perkins pats my arm. "And I have a feeling Alex isn't going to die. Not anytime soon, anyway."

My smile is humongous, I'm sure. "This is the best news ever!"

"Yes it is. However, it comes with a little bad news, I'm afraid. This doesn't change the fact that you told Alex you're a Siren," Grandma Perkins says as she pulls up my driveway. "You've lost your Siren beauty and powers." Wow. Being a Siren was so cool. Going back to my plain ol' self is going to take some getting used to. "Don't look so glum, dear. I'm going to help you get through this." She pats my knee. "Besides, you've still got Roxy beauty and Roxy powers." We get out of the car and start walking up to the front door.

"Thanks, Grandma," I say, taking her hand. "For everything."

She chuckles. "A bowl of Ben and Jerry's is all the thanks I need."

I'm brushing my teeth, trying to avoid seeing myself in the mirror. Not to sound all vain, but it really sucks having to go back to my before-I-was-a-Siren appearance. Kinda like eating McDonald's soft-serve after getting a taste of Ben & Jerry's. Make that half a container. (Grandma Perkins isn't a dainty ice-cream scooper.)

It's a bit weird being in this bathroom right now—the same place where I transformed into a Siren on my birthday. But it's all good, I keep reminding myself. I mean, look at poor Alex, lying in that hospital bed with all those gizmos connected to his body, having to go through who-knows-what after that terrible wreck. Sure, being a Siren was fun and all, but life goes on.

I dig out my brush and try to detangle this rat's nest (a.k.a. my hair), but it's a lost cause. So I get out my acne wash and splash some water on my face. Oh, *great*. Guess I should've taken off my glasses first.

Pumpkin pokes his head through the doorway and yips. "What is it, boy? You don't recognize me, do you?" I pat his head and he growls, backing out of the bathroom like I'm going to pull out that princess doggie costume I force him to wear every Halloween.

When I finally finish fumbling through my get-ready-for-bed routine, Grandma Perkins is waiting in my room, *The Siren Handbook* on her lap.

"How'd you know where I hid it?" I ask, sitting down beside her.

She smiles and shrugs. "I always hid it

in my lingerie drawer. I just had a feeling you'd do the same."

"I guess I won't be needing it anymore." I feel so sad, returning this to my grandma. It meant so much to her that I, too, was a Siren. "I'm so sorry to have disappointed you."

She strokes my frizzy, tangled hair and looks at me with those gorgeous green eyes. "You didn't disappoint me, honey. The whole point of being a Siren is getting what you want. And by giving up your Siren powers, you've gotten exactly what you want. You've found love."

I start crying like a baby. I take off my glasses and dry my tears on my shirt. When I look over at her, tears are falling down her cheeks too.

"To tell you the truth, you've taught me more about being a Siren than I've taught you." Grandma makes a hiccup-y sound and then abruptly stands. "Well, dear, I'm going to go try out that guest room down the hall." She tucks *The Siren Handbook* under her arm and starts for the door.

"See you in the morning," I say.

Grandma Perkins whirls around, wiping the tears off her cheeks and smiling warmly.

She looks like a heroine in a classic romance movie. "I'll take you to the hospital in the morning, dear. Now try to get some sleep."

When I see Pumpkin wandering down the hall, I jump out of bed and grab him. He yaps and wriggles out of my hold. "Don't you want to sleep with me, boy?" I ask. In a fit of whimpers, he scampers down the hall to where Grandma Perkins is spending the night.

Before getting in bed again, I find the biggest, brightest star in the night sky. "I wish that Alex recovers quickly," I whisper. I can't wait to start our new life as "more than friends."

Eighteen

A loud, squeaky yawn wakes me up. Down by my feet, Pumpkin yawns again and stretches his little legs. Guess he had a change of heart. I jump out of bed and rub his cute, pointy ears. "Hey, boy. Glad to see you like hanging out with me again. See? It's not that bad." I open the blinds and look across the street to Alex's house. It's weird being up this early and not seeing his Civic parked on the side of the road.

Hang on.

What's weird is *being able to see without my glasses*!

I run to my bureau mirror and gasp. How can it be that I'm Lindsay-Lohan-eat-your-heart-out gorgeous again? Was losing my Siren beauty just a bad dream? Was it a hallucination brought on by the tragedy of Alex's accident?

"Grandma," I yell. "Wake up!"

I tear through my closet, searching for the perfect first-time-to-see-my-boyfriend-since-he-woke-up-from-a-coma outfit. (If it sounds like a soap opera, I may as well look like I'm starring in one, right?)

There's a soft knock on my bedroom door. "Roxy? Is everything okay?" Grandma Perkins asks, her voice a little sleepy sounding.

"It's better than okay! Come on in and see!"

The door opens slowly. I turn around, my flirty Jaded skirt twirling, and stop mid-spin. "Grandma?"

The woman standing in my room bears a striking resemblance to Grandma Perkins, but something's drastically different. She's no longer beautiful. She's not exactly *ugly*, but she's just so ordinary looking. Oh, God, is my mouth hanging open?

"Um, hi . . . ," I stammer, averting my eyes until I can get a better handle on the situation. What the hell is going on?

"It's okay, Roxy. I know you're probably

surprised to see me like this." She chuckles. "To be honest, I'm having a bit of trouble with my appearance as well. I've never seen myself like this before. I've been a Siren for forty-five years, you know."

Her hair is coarse and a grayish-white color instead of blond. She's the same height, but instead of curves, she's all knees and elbows. Her skin has a reddish under-tone with some wrinkles sprinkled in, and her lashes and brows are sparse. She looks a lot like Mom will probably look twenty years down the road. Actually, she looks a lot more like a *grandmother*.

Grandma Perkins closes the space between us and runs her fingers through my shiny red mane. Tears glisten in her light brown eyes. "You are beautiful, both inside and out."

"But . . . how?" I flail my arms, hope-lessly confused.

She lowers her lanky frame onto the foot of my bed and pats the space beside her for me to sit down. "I didn't tell you last night because I wasn't sure if it would work. These past few days have been so emotional for you, and I really didn't want to get your hopes up for nothing. . . ."

"Grandma, what are you talking about?"

I didn't realize until now that she's holding *The Siren Handbook*. She flicks through until she finds the page she's looking for, and sets it on my lap. "This part of the legend has always intrigued me. You see, when her lover was on his deathbed, Thelxiepia revealed to him that she was a Siren."

"Like me," I whisper.

Grandma Perkins nods solemnly. "Yes, like you. And like you, Thelxiepia lost her Siren powers. Until her elder sister, Pisinoe, asked Hades for a favor." She rests her hand on my back, leaning closer to *The Siren Handbook*. After clearing her throat, she reads out loud: "Her own death forthcoming, Pisinoe beseeched Hades to transfer her Siren powers to Thelxiepia, who, in spite of her impassioned mourning, was full of life. Hades, who had much to gain by the survival of the Sirens, granted Pisinoe this final request."

I shake my head, my fiery hair sweeping over my shoulders. "I still don't get how you transferred your Siren powers to me, though."

Grandma gazes out my window for a

moment before answering. "I just did what Pisinoe did."

My mouth drops open in disbelief. "You talked to the god of the underworld?"

She laughs. "Not exactly."

"Tell me!"

"Well, okay, here goes. But I'd better warn you. It's really *bizarre*, as you say. First I closed my eyes and cleared my head of all extraneous thoughts. Next I concentrated on what a beautiful person you are. I focused on all the wonderful, unselfish things you've done, particularly since becoming a Siren. Then when I couldn't possibly fill my mind with another thought, I took a deep breath, focusing on all the good times I've had as a Siren. And when I exhaled, I envisioned my future without the powers and responsibilities of being a Siren."

She flips to the front of *The Siren Handbook*, running her finger over the picture of the Siren. We're both silent for several minutes. Finally, I speak. "Okay, so that *is* totally bizarre."

Grandma Perkins laughs, and I don't think I imagined that snort. "Yes, it is."

Twenty minutes later Grandma Perkins emerges from the bathroom with her hair and makeup done, dressed in a linen pantsuit and matching heels. She doesn't look Siren-beautiful, but she looks nice. And her eyes may not be emerald green anymore, but they still have their twinkle.

"Roxy, I'm going to go on a trip for a few weeks."

"Where are you going?"

She reaches over to squeeze my cheeks. "Don't worry about me. Now, go get that man of yours!"

"Alex?"

The nurse nods at me as I sidle up to his bed. Patricia is sitting in a beige chair, drumming her fingertips on the armrest. She's watching her son with pure love in her eyes. She shifts her gaze to me and says, "He's been asking for you."

"Mom, can you go five lousy minutes without embarrassing me?" Alex murmurs, his eyelids half-closed and swollen. The bed is angled upward, like the beds at Willington House when the old people are watching TV. He's still puffy-looking, but he's not as red as yesterday. The blood is cleaned off, and bandages and Band-Aids cover his cuts. His skin and hair look so shiny and clean.

"Well, it's the truth," Patricia says. "You *were* asking for her."

The nurse scribbles something on her pad and then slips out of the room.

"Mom? Will you go get me some Sprite or something?" Alex asks.

She stands up. "Of course, honey. I'll take my time." With a wink, Patricia closes the door behind her.

Once we're alone, I put my hand on his and kiss his cheek. "Hey, Rox," he says.

"Hey." After a beat, I say, "So, I've been thinking."

"Uh-oh. Sounds dangerous." He smiles lazily.

"We should definitely keep volunteering. We make the old folks so happy. They have a reason to wake up in the morning, to snap in their dentures and slip on their Depends. And the dogs! We make the dogs happy too. They love being able to get out of their kennels and stretch their legs. We can't give this up, Alex. It's up to us to bring everything together. It's up to us to make a difference. It's up to us—"

"To scoop the dog poop," Alex says.

"Why do you always have to make a joke when I'm trying to be serious?" I put my hands on my hips, pretending to be annoyed.

"I'm sorry. You were saying?"

I intertwine my fingers with his. "God, Alex. I'm just so relieved you're okay. I was so scared I was going to lose you."

"Really? Man, I'm sorry. I'll make it up to you. As soon as they let me out of here, we're having Egg McMuffins. My treat."

"That sounds great."

We're both quiet for a little while, holding hands, just breathing. I hear people out in the hall, their voices muffled behind the door. The fluorescent lights hum softly, and the blinds tremble when the AC turns on.

Alex locks his heavy-lidded eyes with mine. "I had the strangest dream when I was in the coma. You were in it, and you were sitting right here, telling me you were a goddess . . . no, wait. A Siren. Yeah, that's it. And you were explaining how everything you've achieved this summer was because you had these amazing powers. And that truck crashed into me and I was going to die, all because you fell in love with me."

I straighten my posture. "Oh, really?"

His eyelids open a little more, showing those beautiful caramel eyes.

I stroke his cheek and whisper, "Well,

I know one part wasn't just a dream."

"Oh yeah? Which part?"

I lean over and kiss him lightly on the lips. Then I kiss him deeply. His eyes widen. "Hey! I wasn't talking about *that* kind of dream!"

"You're so full of it." I punch him in the arm and he yelps out in pain. "Oh, God! Sorry, Alex."

He scoops up my chin and looks into my emerald green eyes. "I'm glad you're not really a Siren."

I'm not sure what to say, so I just squeeze his hand.

"I want you to love me, but I'd rather not die."

"I love you."

He closes his eyes and makes a loud, obnoxious croaking sound. I start laughing and don't stop until he quits playing dead and kisses me.

On my way home from St. Mary's Hospital a week later, I hear the muffled tune of "Shut Up" and dig into the depths of my Pucci tote. It takes me two years to find the damn thing, this bag is so big. I'm so going back to my Old Navy satchel. It may be cheap and out of style, but at least I know exactly where everything is in it. I hold the phone to my ear.

"How's Alex doing today?" Natalie asks.

"Oh, he's okay. I mean, he's pretty banged up and can hardly stay awake to finish a sentence, but the doctors expect him to make a full recovery. He's going to make it. And that's what matters."

"Are you two engaged yet?"

I snort. "Hel-*lo*? We're only sixteen."

"Fine, then. Have you two done the deed yet?"

"In the hospital?" I ask, mortified that she'd even think that.

She laughs. "Noooo. Before—when he spent the night at your house. You know, the night before the accident?"

"Natalie! That's so none of your business."

"I thought so."

"I didn't say—"

"What*ever*. Anyway, Fuchsia and I are driving up to visit him tonight. Do you want to come?"

"Yeah, cool." I pass a billboard with a Vail Hot-Air Balloon Fest advertisement. A girl I've never seen before is the model, and she looks amazing.

Chase and his buddies are splayed out on the living room floor. Looks like they're watching that *Dukes of Hazzard* movie. "Hey, dork! Get the hell out of the way!" Chase yells at me as I dodge a shower of Barbeque Pringles.

"Nice Mickey Mouse shirt, Chase. Did Dad get you the ears to go with it?"

All's back to normal on the home front.

I venture into the kitchen and find Mom nuking an all-in-one meal. She's wearing a Tinker Bell T-shirt and capris. I grab a Diet Coke out of the fridge and perch on a barstool, waiting for her to get off the phone. She's laughing and sighing and really into her conversation. Who's she talking to?

Five minutes later, after I've finished my drink and helped myself to a nectarine, she says, "Yes, she's here. Oh, really? Well, you know I love surprises. Okay, see you in a little while," and hangs up.

"Who was that?" I ask.

"Mother."

"Oh? So since when do you two talk on the phone?" Okay, so maybe not *every*thing's back to normal.

She nods, smiling wistfully. "After all these years of being so distant, she's suddenly reaching out. It's nice."

Pumpkin scurries into the kitchen and sits up between us, sticking up his little front legs and wagging his tail. "Do we have any more of those doggie cookies you get at the bakery?" I ask, knowing good and well what the little pooch is after.

Mom rummages around in a brown paper sack and presents Pumpkin with his favorite treat. Pumpkin snatches it up and dashes over to the pantry to eat while Mom fills the cookie jar with the remaining treats.

"How's Alex doing, by the way?" Mom asks, her eyes full of sympathy.

"Fine. The doctor thinks he might be ready to go home in another week or two. He should be able to start school with the rest of us."

"That's great. What a horrible accident. He's lucky to be alive."

"I know."

"Oh, I almost forgot. Someone from your talent agency called and wants you to be a hostess at Rob McGee's parking-lot sale Saturday morning."

"Okay, I'll give them a call back." I'll have to decline, seeing as how that's my day to volunteer at the PAD.

Pumpkin starts barking up a storm. I peek out the kitchen window. Sure enough, Grandma's Lexus is creeping up the driveway.

I run out to the front room to greet her. "I brought snickerdoodles," Grandma Perkins says. She's wearing a long gypsy skirt and a wrap blouse. She looks lovely. But seeing her as a non-Siren still floors me. Chase and his friends grab the bag of cookies like it's the latest issue of *Playboy*. "Wait!" She snatches the bag out of Chase's hands, takes out a freakishly large one, and hands it to me. As I take a bite of the cinnamon-sugar cookie, it occurs to me that my grandma is acting like a regular grandma.

"Mother! You're staying for dinner, right?" Mom calls from the kitchen. "It's nothing as fancy as what you're used to, but we'd love to have you."

"It would be my pleasure," she says, setting her mondo Gucci handbag on the tile floor. Then she whispers in my ear, "She hasn't seen me now that I'm not a Siren any longer. Will you be a dear and come with me for moral support?"

I nod and follow Grandma Perkins into the kitchen.

"Hi, Mother," Mom says, drying her

hands on a dish towel and coming at her in hug mode. She stops short and looks Grandma up and down, her brow furrowed. "You look . . . different. Is everything okay? Are you . . . sick?"

Grandma does that new little laugh-snort thing. "Couldn't be better, dear. I just went on a little vacation and got a bit of R and R."

My mouth suddenly dry, I grab the can of soda pop I was drinking earlier and take a quick swig. Only the can is empty, so I get a new one out of the fridge. "Don't you just love her hair, Mom? I was always telling her she should try out the natural look. It's all the rage, you know." I smile at Grandma and see that Mom is smiling too.

"Yes, she looks wonderful," Mom says. "So, what glamorous hot spot did you go to this time?"

Grandma's gaze lowers, making her look almost bashful. "Nebraska."

I start choking and Diet Coke comes through my nose. Ow! (Warning: Don't try this at home.) "What the heck for?" I ask when I get ahold of myself.

"Well," Grandma says, settling herself onto a barstool. "I wanted to get something special for your mother."

The doorbell chimes. Grandma taps her Cartier watch, her eyes twinkling. "Ah, right on time. Well, Merrilee, are you just going to stand there, or are you going to answer the door?"

Mom gives us a weird look and then heads for the foyer. "What is it?" I whisper to Grandma as we follow Mom.

"You'll see."

Mom swings open the door and just stares at whomever's on the other side. Finally, she says, "Can I help you?"

"Merrilee?" a man's voice asks.

Then Grandma Perkins steps in. "Merrilee, this is your father."

Oh my God! This is crazy!

Mom looks at Grandma and then looks at the man, tears welling up in her eyes.

"Are you going to invite him in?" I ask, tagging on a nonverbal *hint, hint*.

Mom laughs. "Of course, how silly of me! Sorry, I'm just, well, um, this is quite the surprise, is all. . . ."

As her father (my grandfather!) comes inside and introduces himself as Harvey VandenHout, it's obvious they're related. I mean, he's got the same brown frizzy hair and the same pale skin. He's about six feet tall and, by the size of his biceps, obviously works out. You know, he's actually quite handsome for an old guy. And what's more, he and Grandma make an adorable couple.

"Why don't you two start getting acquainted?" Grandma says, escorting them into the living room. Once my mom and her father are sitting down, Grandma gestures for me to come with her. I take her arm and she leads me to my bedroom.

"Really, Roxy. You should keep your room cleaner than this. This is disgusting."

"Yeah, I know. I'll work on it." More like, I'll use my Siren powers on Chase again. He was such a fabulous room-cleaner. "So, what's the story, Grandma? How'd you find Harvey?"

"I've known where he lives all along." She sighs and plops down on my bed. I sit down beside her. "It's just that I was afraid to bring him back into my life because I was afraid of falling in love with him. But you already know that."

"And now that you're not a Siren anymore, you are free to fall in love!"

"That's right, dear. But first and foremost, I did it for your mom. You were right. It wasn't fair to keep her father a secret from her. She deserves to know him. He's a wonderful, wonderful man."

"And kinda cute, too," I say, playfully elbowing her in her ribs.

"Oh, yes. He's aged very nicely indeed!"

"And I'm sure he's thinking the same about you."

We giggle and then hug.

"Gertrude! Roxy! I'm supposed to tell you dinner's ready," Dad calls from the hallway.

"Be right there!" I say.

"But first . . ." Grandma reaches into her handbag and pulls out a gift box. "This is for you, dear."

I take off the bow and stick it on my head, and then rip the paper off. Oh my God. It's a Barbie. And not just any Barbie, it's "Band Girl" Barbie. I open the box and take her out. She even comes with a music stand, sheet music, and an instrument case. I pry the little black case apart, and inside is a miniature silver flute.

"Happy belated birthday, Roxy."

I'm sitting under a tree in my front yard, winding an elastic band around my hair in a makeshift ponytail, when Natalie's yellow

Sportage pulls up the driveway. It's a gorgeous mid-August morning, with just a scattering of puffy clouds in the otherwise clear sky. A perfect day for walking dogs.

"Can you believe school starts in just four days?" Natalie asks, passing me a piece of cinnamon gum as soon as I'm in the car. She's wearing an adorable newsboy hat and an orange-blue-and-khaki-plaid skirt.

"It's been a crazy summer, that's for sure," I say from the backseat. And I have a feeling it's going to be an even crazier school year. I'm just glad I have my old group of friends to hang out with.

And I'm psyched to have such an amazing boyfriend.

Natalie reverses onto the street and then coasts to Alex's house. He's waiting on the stoop, and when he sees us coming, he stands up and starts making his way across the lawn.

I'm on an emotional roller coaster as I watch Alex's slow progress. First a swell of love for him, then sadness that he's still in so much pain. Finally, waves of happiness and relief overtake me, because, you know what? It could've been a lot worse.

Cautiously, Alex clambers into the shotgun seat. He gives Natalie a peck on her cheek and then turns back and gives my outreached hand a squeeze.

For pretty much the entire fifteen-minute drive to the Pet Advocacy of Denver, Natalie fills our ears with play-by-plays of how Eva came into Jaded and bought hundreds of dollars' worth of new back-to-school clothes. ". . . And while I was ringing her up, she kept gushing about what a gift I have for putting outfits together, and these two girls who look exactly like the Olsen twins overheard, and before I knew it, they were requesting me as their personal shopper!"

"Awesome," I say when she pauses to catch her breath.

"But that's not all!" Natalie exclaims, pulling into the PAD parking lot. "Sebastian heard the whole thing, and guess what?"

Alex turns back to me and I give him an exaggerated shrug.

"He's promoting you to manager?" Alex asks.

Natalie pauses, considering this. "No. But he *is* giving me a fifty-cent raise!"

"We should go to Murphy's to celebrate," I say. "Natalie's treat, since she's the one raking it in."

"Okay, I'll be your sugar mama, but you remember this when you're a famous model, girl."

After Alex and I jump out of her car, Natalie waves and leaves for her shift at Jaded.

The Willington House van driver and one of the PAD volunteers are assisting the six women and a Hawaiian-shirted Benjamin as they gradually unload and line up on the sidewalk. A true tour de force, considering all the canes and walkers.

When the old people spot us, some of them wave and some just smile. Except for Rosie, who's frowning deeply, her wrinkles pooling on her chin. Looks like she's her grumpy self today. After we greet everybody and introduce ourselves to the four non-regulars, Alex and I lead the colorful poly-ester parade along the narrow pathway to the PAD's backyard.

Alex must've noticed Rosie's sour mood too, because he stops to wait for her. "Rosie, what's the deal? Aren't you happy to see us?" he asks, holding his arm out to her and escorting her toward the paved walkway.

Her brightly rouged cheeks twitch, but she doesn't smile. "Of course, Alexander.

I'm tickled pink that you're all right. And I'm glad Roxy has become such a beautiful young woman. But, you see, Deana made me wear these walking shoes and I don't like them one bit."

"They look comfy," Alex says, plainly trying to console her. But I sense a storm, so I hold back in case he needs help.

"Exactly!" she shouts. "That's the problem. Shoes aren't supposed to look comfortable. And furthermore, they don't go with my pants. Whoever heard of wearing white walking shoes with black slacks?"

"Well, Rosie, if anyone can pull it off, it's you. Your blouse is lovely," I say into her good ear, gesturing at her black-and-white floral shirt. "Very fashionable. And I'm sure you have a killer shoe collection, but there will be plenty of other opportunities to wear them."

She sighs loudly, her grimace unyielding. "Yes, I suppose so."

"What's this, Rosie?" Eleanor says in her low, scratchy voice. "You butterin' up these kids so they'll let you walk the poodle this time?" She winks at Alex and me.

"You got him last time," Rosie says through pursed lips.

Now Benjamin has caught up to us. He taps his walker by Rosie's white sneakers and says, "Neither of ya got the cotton-pickin' poodle last time. He was adopted." Benjamin starts walking away, muttering, "Damn women, can't remember nothin'. . . ."

Eleanor's dark brown eyes glisten. "Adopted? What a lucky dog!"

"I know how he feels," Alex whispers in my ear as he wraps his arm around my waist. I can't help but blush.

Alex and I wait until everybody makes it to the section of benches by the walkway, and then we head inside the building to help the PAD folks leash today's dogs. He takes my hand in his, and a zing of electricity zaps through my body.

"So, how does it feel?" Alex asks.

"It makes me want to run back behind that bush over there and do more than just hold hands," I blurt.

He gives me this really weird look and I bite my lower lip. Have I said something wrong? Am I being too forward? Is there a rewind button?

Alex's eyebrows eventually return to their normal position and he lets out a big laugh. "I was talking about being back at the PAD."

I'm totally speechless. Thank goodness Roberto, the PAD director, interrupts this moment of extreme awkwardness by bringing out the dogs.

"Get back here!" Roberto cries over all the barking and yipping. Though the dogs are leashed, they're yanking the husky man across the lawn like he's nothing more than a blowup dummy. Alex lunges forward, trying to grab as many dogs as possible by the collars. But the dogs break free from him, and Roberto can't hold the leashes any longer.

They're. Heading. Straight. For. Me.

Alex and Roberto watch in stunned silence as the dogs form a circle around my feet, tails wagging, tongues hanging. I look behind me, and, sure enough, the folks from Willington House are staring in disbelief. How the heck am I going to explain *this*?

"Must be my new perfume," I say with a nervous laugh, trying to shake a little white terrier off my leg.

To my relief, Alex nods as if he gets it. "That's some perfume!"

"Well, it's just something that I picked up at—"

Before I can babble another word, Alex puts his hands on my shoulders and steers me over to the bush—the one I was talking about jumping him behind. The dogs follow in Pied Piper fashion.

"So what's going on, really?" Alex asks softly, so no one besides me can hear. "I know it's not perfume, Rox."

I sigh. "Okay, you got me. I thought I could get away with it, but you're too smart a cookie." I reach into my satchel and pull out a paper bag, swaying it in front of Alex's face.

He snatches the bag and peeks inside.

"Gourmet doggie cookies," I inform him.

Grinning, Alex tosses the treats high into the air. The dogs scatter in every direction, chasing and catching the cookies.

Alex cradles my head in his hands and pulls me in for a delicious kiss. The kiss lasts for an eternity, but it's not nearly long enough.

As time passed, Thelxiepia's womb grew large with the sailor's child. This daughter, upon reaching the age of womanhood, found herself not only a creature of spellbinding beauty, but of musical mastery and great power. It is in this way that the legacy of the Siren shall live on, as it does in you.

About the Author

Wendy Toliver earned her BA in speech communication/broadcast from Colorado State University. She's explored a variety of jobs, from impersonating Marilyn Monroe for singing telegrams to impersonating a computer geek at an advertising agency. Now she calls Eden, Utah, home and lives with her husband, her three little boys, two dogs, a cat, and an occasional mole. When not working on her next novel, Wendy enjoys reading, skiing, snowboarding, acting, volunteering, and traveling. Visit her online at www.wendytoliver.com.

LOL at this sneak peek of

Love, Hollywood Style
By P.J. Ruditis

A new Romantic Comedy from Simon Pulse

"I think I'm in a funk," I said.

"A generic funk or something specific?"

"A guy funk," I said, taking a bite out of my salad.

"Ah," she said.

"There seems to be a pattern developing," I said, finally forcing myself to deal with the thing I'd been avoiding for weeks. "I D-Q'd Dairy Queen guy, slammed the book on the worm I met at Barnes & Noble, and couldn't even find an interesting way to describe how boring the dude from the surf shop was. All before we even got to a second date."

"You *have* been going on a lot of first dates lately," Liz said. "Not to say there's anything wrong with serial dating."

"Except for all the Fruit Loops you meet along the way," I said. Like she knew anything about serial dating. She was a serial monogamist. The queen of relationships all through middle school and high school. At the start of every school year, she'd begin dating a new guy. It would be months of bliss, until about mid-April when the guy realized that— after spending every weekend hiking through the Santa Monica mountains, skiing in Big Bear, and dirt-bike riding in the desert—going out with Liz could be exhausting.

Every guy she ever dated tended to break up with her before the year was out. She kept saying how she didn't mind since she liked to take the summers for herself, but I knew that she was ready for a serious *long*, long-term thing, even though she hadn't even turned eighteen yet.

I understood how she felt. I'd never had a real relationship before. Sure, I'd had boyfriends. I'd been going out with a real sweet guy named Scott at the start of senior year. He was the longest relationship I'd ever had, and we didn't even make it to Christmas. After a while we both realized there was no spark and ended it . . . blandly.

The first-date syndrome seemed to be a recent development. In my post-Scott world I was so busy getting ready to graduate from high school and start my life that guys always seemed to take the backseat. It was almost like I would give up on a date before I'd even started, because none of those guys seemed to fit my picture for the future. I wasn't in some great rush to settle down or anything, but I wasn't really seeing the point of random dating when everything else I was doing was planning for the long term. Not that I had any clue what my life held in store for me beyond college. I hadn't even settled on a major yet.

"If only these dates were more . . . well, just more," I said.

"Not every first date can be a candlelit dinner at the Griffith Park Observatory," Liz said.

"True," I agreed with a sigh.

Liz was talking about what my parents did on their first date. Dad was an astronomy student at the time. He'd given up an entire month of his life to help one of his professors rewrite the manuscript for a textbook about the universe. The professor's editors had hated the first draft.

After Dad gave it the once-over, it was accepted by the publisher and much congratulations were heaped on the professor for the amazing work he'd done revising it. The professor thanked Dad by getting him access to the famous Griffith Park Observatory after hours so he could take the woman who would one day become my mom there on a date. Spending an evening alone together looking at the cosmos is a pretty impressive way to start off a relationship.

And it was just the inspiration I needed.

"I think it's time I fell in love," I declared, slamming down my bottle of Sobe tea to punctuate the statement. It felt like the moment required a dramatic action. We *were* at a movie studio after all.

"Always a good way to pass the time," Liz agreed with a smile. That smile dropped when she saw the look on my face and realized I was being serious. "Tracy?"

"Hear me out," I said. "I'm spending so much time thinking about the future that I'm missing out on the present. And the thing I've been missing out on most is a good guy. I've got to stop worrying about all that future stuff and just let myself fall in love."

Liz nodded. "Okay, yes, that's a good point," she said. "But should falling in love really be a goal? It's not something to put on a to-do list."

"You know what I mean," I said. "I don't have to worry about school until the fall. I don't have to worry about my future until after that. I can spend my summer finding the perfect love."

Liz cocked her ear like she was listening for something.

"What are you doing?" I asked.

"Waiting for the music to swell," she said. "If this were a movie, this would be the point where the sappy romantic music hits a crescendo."

I flicked a sesame seed at her.

"Ladies!" a familiar male voice said from behind me.

"Hey, bro!" I said as Dex sat beside me. Technically, he was Liz's brother, but I'd been calling him "bro" since before I found out it was actually lame to call anyone "bro," and it kind of stuck. "Thanks for the light effects earlier. The tourists got a kick out of it."

"Any time," he said with a smile. "Now maybe you can help *me*. I've got a bet with the guys on the light crew. I need to know what the first movie to win the Academy Award for Best Picture was. They're telling me it was a Sovereign Studios film."

"Ha!" Liz and I spat out in unison. Even in its earliest days, Sovereign Studios was never known for quality films. Huge money-making blockbusters? Yes. But award-winning works of art? Not even.

"I've got a case of Jones soda riding on it," Dex said. "Bubble gum flavor."

"Eww," I said, sticking out my tongue. "Too sweet."

"Thanks," he said. "You're sweet too."

I smacked him on the shoulder. Dex was actually the first of the Sanchez siblings that I had met back in kindergarten. He and Liz are twins. They look a lot alike actually, with the same straight black hair and green eyes, and this beautifully tanned skin they get along with their Mexican heritage.

Dex and I probably would have become best friends the moment he offered me his chocolate milk on the first day. I mean, come on, he was gifting me with chocolate! But he was a yucky boy so it was only natural that Liz and I would be friends while he followed us around pretending to hate us.

"Wait a minute," Liz said. "A bunch of union guys made a bet for bubble gum—flavored soda?"

Dex blushed. "Well . . . if they win I give them beer money. If I win I get bubble gum soda."

His sister tried her best not to laugh. She failed.

Dex is only an apprentice in the studio's

lighting department since he just got out of high school. He's not a full-scale union guy, but he doesn't really want to be doing that for the rest of his life like most of his coworkers have been. He'd much rather be an actor. Dex took the job because his dad works on the studio's light crew and Dex needed the money for college. The guys are always making fun of him because he's so young.

"You know the answer, right?" Dex asked.

I stole a french fry off his plate. "The first film to win an Academy Award was *Wings*. It was produced by Paramount Pictures in 1927."

Dex gave his fist a pump in the air. "Yes! I can't wait to tell those guys. I will totally split the soda with you."

"That's okay," I said. *Really.*

"So, what was the topic of conversation before I got here?"

"Tracy and her guy problems," Liz said casually.

"Liz!" I shouted through clenched teeth. Luckily the teeth clenching and the volume of the conversations around us kept my voice from carrying.

"What?" Liz asked, all innocent-like. "If you can't talk to your brother-substitute about guy troubles, who can you talk to?"

But I wasn't about to talk to anyone about anything, because at that very moment the door to the commissary opened and *he* walked in.

If my life were a movie, this would be the part where the film went into slow motion as the dusty blond–haired, blue-eyed, stylishly-dressed-in-a-suit-two-levels-above-his-pay-grade guy of my dreams entered the picture: Connor Huxley.

Connor was a summer intern in the motion picture marketing department. I'd met him when I gave the orientation tour on his first day at the studio. Every Monday a tour guide takes the new employees around to give them a little background on the studio and point out the necessary places, like the commissary, credit union, infirmary——that kind of thing. Sovereign Studios covers over seventy-five acres in the heart of Hollywood so it's not like your typical office place. New employees can get lost just looking for a bathroom.

During the one hour mini-tour, I learned that Connor was going into his sophomore year at USC as a marketing major. We hit it off pretty well in spite of the fact that I was about to start at UCLA in the fall, which made us natural enemies because of our rival school choices.

We'd both been so busy with our summer

jobs that we'd hardly talked since then, other than saying "Hi" as we passed while I was giving a tour or he was running an errand. A couple of times I thought he was going to ask me out, but then a tourist interrupted, or he got a call from his boss on his cell phone and had to run off. I thought about asking him out too, but considering how unlucky I'd been with love lately, I didn't see the point.

"Where did she go?" Dex asked, waving his hand in front of my face.

"I don't know," Liz replied. "But she always goes there when Connor's around."

I had a sneaking suspicion that they were talking about me. "Excuse me?"

"You're all dreamy-eyed," Liz said.

"I am *not* dreamy-eyed," I replied, blinking pointedly at her. "I was thinking."

"About *Coooonnor*," Liz said in a singsong voice that made both Dex and me roll our eyes.

"Him again?" Dex asked. He always hated when we got all girly, talking about guys. I guess there are some subjects guys are uncomfortable about hearing from their sisters—or sister-substitutes.

"Abrupt subject switch," I announced, hoping to derail the topic of conversation before it got started. "Do we know how long this movie's supposed to run? I don't want to be stuck on VIP transport all night."

"You got shuttle duty?" Liz asked. "That sucks."

"One of the biggest movie premieres of the summer and I'm stuck driving the guests back and forth from the theater to the dining room all night, and I don't even get to see the movie."

"But you probably get to meet celebs," Dex said. "Maybe hang with Christy Caldwell."

"Ha!" Liz and I said—again—in unison. We'd both done VIP transport before. We knew full well that shuttle duty was the last place anyone got to interact with the glamorous glitterati.

"The celebrities all get personal handlers escorting them," I explained to Dex. "Shuttle duty is for the executives who think they're somebody—"

"Well, technically, they *are* somebody," Liz said. "They do kind of run the studio."

"What are you doing for the premiere?" Dex asked his biological sister.

"Ushering," she replied. "Which means I'm stuck inside watching this drivel."

Dex shook his head. "What is it with you

two? We get to work at Sovereign Studios, one of the oldest motion picture and TV lots in Hollywood." He looked at me. "You're going to be rubbing elbows with some of the biggest power players in town—"

"More like carting their butts around."

He turned to his sister. "And you're going to be one of the first people in the world to see what everyone is saying will be the blockbuster romantic comedy of the summer. You are both way too young to be so jaded."

"When did he become the voice of reason?" I asked Liz.

"Always been that way," Liz replied. "It's damn annoying."

Dex was right, though. And we weren't seriously upset about working the premiere. We just like to whine sometimes. It was kind of exciting to be involved in a big movie premiere with movie stars and the Hollywood elite—even if I was nothing more than a second-rate chauffeur. But you never want to *look* like you're excited about those things. That would be tacky.

Jaded is the Hollywood version of excitement.

"Are you sticking around for the premiere?" I asked Dex.

"Can't," he said. "I've got an audition for a play in a little theater on Santa Monica."

"Break a leg," I said. I wanted to ask him more about it, but Dex didn't like talking about roles until he had them. Like everyone else in Hollywood, Dex had aspirations for something beyond his day job. Well, like everyone but me. I still wasn't sure what I wanted to be when I grew up, but I knew that tour guide was not a career option. At least Dex wasn't going the typical route of being a waiter while he pursued his acting dreams.

"Hey," Liz said. "Here comes lover boy again."

I willed myself not to look up from my salad, but I could see Liz's body shift as she turned toward the kitchen. I silently repeated to myself, *Don't look. Don't look.* But the salad could only hold my interest for so long.

My head popped up to catch a glimpse of Connor as he elbowed his way out the door of the commissary. He was loaded down with about a half dozen to-go containers, heading back to the office with his bosses' meals, I guessed. I bet I'd see him at the premiere later.

Suddenly, my outlook on the event was a lot less jaded.